JUST LIKE EVERYONE ELSE

For Esther and Miriam, super readers and super writers.

First published in the UK in 2023 by Usborne Publishing Limited., Usborne House, 83-85 Saffron Hill, London EC1N 8RT, England. usborne.com

Usborne Verlag, Usborne Publishing Limited., Prüfeninger Str. 20, 93049 Regensburg, Deutschland, VK Nr. 17560

A CIP catalogue record for this book is available from the British Library.

ISBN 9781801315784 7698/1 JFM MJJASOND/23

Printed and bound using 100% renewable energy at CPI Group (UK) Ltd, Croydon, CR0 4YY.

SARAH HAGGER-HOLT

JUST LIKE EVERYONE ELSE

Four years earlier

The first time I ran away from home, I was nine years old. And no one noticed.

I didn't want to run away, not really. I just wanted to *be* away. Just for a little while. I wanted to feel like I was the only person in the world, not swallowed up by all the people and the noise and the busyness at home.

I was allowed to go to Jack's house up the road or to the shop on the corner by myself, but I always had to tell Mum or Dad where I was going. No argument.

But that day, I didn't tell anyone.

Mum had discovered Evie and Daisy drawing on the bathroom wall. It was impossible to know which of them started it – whenever one of them did something, the other always joined in. Mum was trying to prise the pens out of their sticky little fingers as she explained in her "calm voice" why paper, not walls, was for writing on. All the while, Bells was screaming about how those were her new pens, the special ones she got for her birthday, and now they were spoiled. Dad was at work and, because it was Saturday, none of the kids that Mum child-minds during the week was there. And Chloe? I don't know where Chloe was. She's always hated people shouting. She was probably tucked away in a corner with a picture book, waiting in her small, serious way for things to settle down.

I needed to get away. I took a deep breath as the back gate clicked shut behind me. Everything was suddenly quiet.

I didn't have a plan. I started walking up the street, past Jack's house, past the shop, before crossing the road very carefully, looking right and then left and then right again about a hundred times.

Up the top of the hill, there's a field that slopes away from the streets, down to the allotments. It's the best place to sledge in the winter and you can see over the whole of the city right to the hills on the other side. I guess it must have a name, but we always just call it the Field.

Once I reached the Field, I began to speed up. I raced downhill, arms held out on either side like I was flying. The wind on my face, my legs stretched, my feet pressing against the ground, pushing me onwards. I kept going once I reached the footpath at the bottom. It didn't matter where I ran to. Running – that was the important thing, that made me feel free.

I ran until my chest was sore and my legs felt heavy. All I could hear was the blood rushing in my ears and my own breathing. There was no one around, apart from one old guy walking his dog. I felt amazing.

I walked back along the path, trudged up the Field and then slowly back home, no idea how long I'd been gone.

I didn't want to run away any more, what I really wanted was some of Mum's cake, if my sisters hadn't eaten it all already.

My heart was pounding as I climbed onto the bins so I could reach over and open the gate into the garden. I was all ready for a telling-off from Mum for going off without asking and worrying her to death.

But all I could hear was Bells organizing the others into one of her complicated games. I could hardly open the door to the living room, the floor was so covered in cushions and duvets. Chloe sat piling up balled socks into neat stacks, while the twins knocked them down and threw the socks at each other.

"Aidan, tell them to stop," Bells shouted over at me. "They're not allowed to do that yet. They can't throw the ammunition till we've finished making the fort. Mum's no good, she says she doesn't care what we do as long as we leave her in peace for five minutes."

I sat down next to Bells, smiling because I was happy to be home. "Any cake left?" I asked.

The second time I run away, it's different. Then, everybody notices when I'm gone.

May

Chapter One

I pile three Weetabix into a bowl, pause, and then add another one. Why not? Earlier this morning, while everyone else was still getting out of bed, I'd already been running. I train every Saturday morning and once a week after school. I open the fridge to get out the milk. Every shelf is packed full of meat. Of course, I almost forgot, it's today.

Every year, on the first Saturday of May half-term, we have a barbecue. Not just any barbecue but, as Dad always says, the biggest and best barbecue in the whole of Sheffield. It's also the safest barbecue in the whole of Sheffield. Dad's a firefighter and is always telling us stories about things that have gone wrong with other people's barbecues – trees or clothes catching fire, grills being knocked over – things that he'd never let happen at ours.

This barbecue is special – it's a Taylor family tradition. It means that summer has started.

Dad comes into the kitchen, whistling, and slaps me on the back. I choke on my Weetabix.

"Come on, Ade, get moving. I need your help out 'ere, son. Time's moving on."

"Mmph," I say, still coughing. "Get Bells to do it. I need a shower, I've just come back from running. Anyway, no one's coming for hours."

"Bells is *already* helping," says Dad. "And Chloe. But we need all hands on deck. Team Taylor, remember."

"It's just a barbecue...no big deal... " I say to wind Dad up.

"What?" he shouts. "*Just* a barbecue? Just? It's *just* the biggest and best—"

"Barbecue in the whole of Sheffield." I finish for him. "Yeah, I know."

"Well then," says Dad. "Good. Now, shift yourself. And don't be so cheeky. You know people fight over invitations to an event like this. It's like one of them royal garden parties."

"Yeah right."

Dad's already wearing the apron that we got specially printed for him for his birthday. It says "Team Taylor: Captain and Barbecuer-in-Chief" in white on a black background. It was Bells's idea. Of course.

"Anyway, how was running this morning? Good turnout?"

"Yeah, not bad, lots of downhill today. All about building up speed."

"Rather you than me. Now, I've got a challenge for you, do you reckon you could be that fast at making me a cup of tea?"

"Ha ha," I say, but I still get up and put the kettle on for him.

Mum comes in, holding her phone in one hand and a bowl of potato salad in the other. She gives me a kiss as she passes. I shrug her off. Why is it impossible in this family to have five minutes without anybody touching you? I should be grateful that one of the twins hasn't come in and sat on me yet, although they probably will before I finish my breakfast.

Mum wrinkles up her nose. "I hope you're planning to have a shower before people start arriving," she says to me.

"Yes," I sigh. "I am. But when I got home, Daisy was in the bathroom, and now I'm making Dad a cup of tea. If some people wouldn't keep asking me questions and getting me to do stuff while I'm trying to eat my breakfast, then I'd be in the shower already."

"Okay, point taken, sorry," says Mum soothingly.

I look up and see her mouthing "hormones" at Dad over my head.

"It is *not* hormones…" I start to say.

"Never mind," says Mum, putting down the potato salad on the table in front of me. "Listen, Pete, Jo's bringing someone. She's just texted. Is that okay?"

Auntie Jo is Mum's younger sister and one of my favourite people in the whole world. She lives by herself in a fancy flat in the city centre, where everything is smooth and neat, and there's a sofa that she folds out into a bed when I come and stay. She never asks annoying questions about school or whether I've got a girlfriend yet or anything like that. She just talks to me the same as she would to anyone else. She works in marketing. When I was little, I used to think that meant she had a stall down the market, selling veg or something, till Mum laughed and told me it didn't mean that at all. Instead, she works on her laptop, helping companies sell things online.

"Of course she can bring someone," says Dad. "More the merrier. Who is it? A bloke?"

"I *think* so," says Mum, grinning. "She hasn't said, but I think it must be. I've got a feeling."

"About time," says Dad. "She's what, thirty-three now? Clock's ticking. She deserves to find the right guy. And, she should have no trouble, I mean, she's such a looker."

Mum pushes Dad gently, pretending to be offended.

"Not nearly as gorgeous as you, of course," he adds. I can feel my ears going red. I gulp down my final mouthful of Weetabix.

"What if she doesn't *want* a boyfriend?" I say, standing up. My voice comes out high and squeaky and then drops low. I hate it when it does that. It's happening more and more, especially when I get upset or annoyed. "What if she *likes* living by herself, and not having to change nappies all the time and look after boring babies? Have you thought of that?"

I don't stick around long enough to see Mum raise her eyebrows at Dad, or Dad smile back at her. But I know they will.

"Oi, what about that cuppa?" shouts Dad after me. But I hear him opening the cupboard where the mugs are, so I know he's finishing making it himself.

But I'm right, I tell myself, as the hot water flows down my back. I'm right. Just because *they're* married with kids and all their friends are married with kids doesn't mean everyone else has to, or wants to, be like that. It's like they can't imagine anyone wanting anything different.

There are no dry towels. I nearly trip over a box of old plastic bath toys that someone's left on the floor, trying to get one out of the cupboard.

There's a hammering on the door.

"It's my turn, come on," shouts Chloe. "You've been ages."

I wrap the towel round my waist and open the door. At least I got in before Chloe. *She's* the one who spends ages in there, not me, usually perched on the loo seat reading a book. She's only eight and already she's read loads more than me. It's like when she's reading she can shut out all the noise around her and disappear into her own private world. I wish that worked for me too.

Chloe's standing right outside the bathroom. She slips past me the moment I step out of the door. I can hear Bells thundering up the stairs. I'm not sure if she's after me or after getting in the bathroom, but either way, she's too late. I slam my bedroom door shut and push a chair, weighed down with piles of clothes, behind it so that Bells can't just barge in. The one good thing about having four sisters and being the only boy is that I don't have to share a room with anyone.

I could happily stay in my room all day today. I'd miss the food – Dad's barbecue sauce is amazing – and hanging out with Jack, I suppose. But there's always tons of leftovers and I can see Jack any day.

At times like this, I wonder if I'm adopted. I'm just not like Mum or Dad. They thrive on having people around all the time. It makes them bigger and brighter and more themselves when other people are there. Maybe that's why they decided to have five kids, so someone's always around.

Not me, it just tires me out, all the chat and the smiling. It's like I'm a phone and my battery drains a little bit more every person I talk to, until I shut down. But Mum and Dad don't get that.

I never wonder for long about being adopted. All I have to do is look in the mirror at my sticky-out ears and compare them to Bells's and Chloe's and Evie's and Daisy's – and Dad's. Those are some powerful genes.

My phone vibrates. It's Jack, messaging to say that he's just coming round. Which means that he'll arrive in exactly one minute and twenty-five seconds – the time it takes to walk from his house to mine. Walk. Jack never runs because he thinks anything remotely to do with exercise is a waste of time.

I quickly throw on some clothes, find a pair of socks on the floor which don't smell too bad and kind of match, shut the door firmly then put a chair in front of it to discourage lost guests from wandering into my room, looking for the bathroom.

By the time I get downstairs, Jack's already in the kitchen, chatting to Mum and Bells about who's coming to the barbecue. Sometimes it seems like he's more Team Taylor than I am, like he's part of the family. Although I suppose he is.

Jack grew up here. The first kid Mum looked after when she started child-minding. Three days a week from his first birthday to when we started school – Jack had his lunch and tea here, went on walks down the park or came to toddler group with me and Mum, napped in a cot upstairs next to mine, did finger-painting at our kitchen table.

Mum minded other kids too, back then, but none of them was like Jack. I always had the idea that it was my job to look after Jack, not just Mum's. I guess I've never stopped feeling that way. It's just not so straightforward now. Jack's always been a little bit different. It's tricky to say how exactly. His clothes are just a bit more unusual, his laugh a bit louder, the way he walks a little bouncier, than anyone else's. All things that make you stand out at school, that could make you a target. When I ask him why he doesn't just try and blend in a bit more, he just smiles, says it's all cool, and tells me to stop worrying.

Mum looks up as I come in and checks me over with a quick glance. She nods, satisfied that I'm clean and presentable now.

"Jack, Ade, your dad needs a couple of strong lads to

shift round some of the furniture in the garden. You two up for the job?"

"I reckon so," says Jack.

Just as Bells says, "Why's it have to be strong *lads*? That's sexist. I'm as strong as Jack, aren't I? Stronger. I mean, look at his tiny muscles compared to mine." And she leans over to squeeze his arm.

She's probably right too. Jack's skinny and not that well-built. Mr Evans, our sarcastic PE teacher, once described him in front of everyone as a "delicate bloom". It made all the boys laugh, but Jack didn't even blush. Just shrugged it off. It was me who worried for him, anxious about what someone might say about him next.

But I wasn't only worried about him. I was worried what they might say about me too, just for being his friend.

Bells's comment doesn't bother him now, the way it would if someone said that about me. Instead, Jack plays up, flexing his muscles, then challenging Bells to do the same.

Mum shrugs. "If you *really* want to help with moving chairs, Bells, then don't let me stop you." So all three of us go to help Dad. We take turns sneaking handfuls of crisps from the bowl on the table till he spots us, pretends to be cross, and tells us to get out from under his feet.

Before long, the sun's blazing down and the garden's full. Dad's mates from work, the families of the kids that Mum's minded over the years and more families that she knows from being a parent-governor at the primary school. The music's pumping out, everyone's shouting their hellos and laughing too loudly at too many bad jokes. The cans of Coke and beers are disappearing fast.

"You all right?" asks Jack.

"Yeah, just all these people, you know."

"We could just go and play Xbox inside," he suggests.

"Nah." It's tempting, but I know he'd rather be here at the party. "Let's get a burger."

Suddenly I hear my name over the chatter. "Where's Aidan? I've got some news for him."

I spot Auntie Jo before she spots me. She looks a hundred times more glamorous than anyone else here. I tap her on the shoulder and she spins round, then air-kisses me on both cheeks. I like it because it feels like a very grown-up sort of greeting. Even if it's still a bit embarrassing.

"What news?" I ask, excited.

Then I wonder straight away if it's actually something boring, the sort of thing that only adults think is interesting. Maybe it's just about this bloke that Mum and Dad were talking about. That would be a big let-down.

"Here, let me show you." She gets her phone out of her

handbag, unlocks it and passes it over to me. It takes me a minute to read the email and take in what it says.

"No way!" I say. "No way, that's brilliant. You really got in?"

"Yup," she smiles. "At last. I got fed up of never getting anything in the ballot, so I'm running for charity. Now the real work begins. Hope I'm up to it."

"Course you are, easy. Anyway, I'll train with you." I stop, perhaps I'm getting too carried away. "I mean, only if you'd like."

"Of *course* I'd like that, you daft kid." She pulls a serious face. "Although I wasn't sure if you'd want to be seen training with me, I mean I know you don't think this is *real* running, but—" She laughs. Auntie Jo and I always wind each other up about running. She's a road runner, I'm a fell runner. I tease her that she's soft, and she mocks me for how often I come home soaking wet and covered in mud.

"What *are* you two talking about?" asks Jack.

"Auntie Jo's got a place in next year's London Marathon," I tell him. Even people, like Jack, who don't care about running, will get how exciting this is. If I could run any road race in the world, it would be that one. Only six years till I'm old enough.

"Are you going to dress up?" Jack asks. "You know, like

those people who run it dressed as Big Ben or a zebra or something? You could get in the *Guinness Book of Records* that way. That would be so cool."

"Hmm," says Auntie Jo, pretending to consider it. "I *could*. But I think running twenty-six miles will be hard enough without a huge, heavy costume as well, don't you? I am running for charity though – new equipment for the maternity unit at the hospital."

"Well, that's your costume sorted then," says Jack, clapping his hands together. "You've got to run dressed up as a giant baby! Like with a nappy, and carrying a baby's bottle – you could put energy drinks in there – and—"

"Jack…" I interrupt, trying to get him to shut up. But Auntie Jo just laughs.

"Why the hospital?" I ask.

"Well, our family's kept that unit pretty busy over the years, haven't we? I mean, you lot were all born there. Luckily, you were all healthy, even with the twins being early, but imagine what it's like for a family with a baby that's sick and needs special help. Terrible. Anyway, they had running places and it seemed like such a good cause. I hope you'll come to London and cheer me on."

"Seriously?"

"Sure, why not?"

"I don't know. What if Dad's working that weekend?"

I look at my shoes. "And anyway, wouldn't it be a lot of money for all seven of us to go down to London?"

Auntie Jo puts her hand on my shoulder. "I'll talk to your mum. I'm sure we can make it work, okay? After all, it's nearly a whole year away. Plenty of time to plan."

I nod. I hope she's right. It would be brilliant, but such a hassle too. Just imagine trying to get the twins on and off the tube without them losing something or having to stop every five minutes for someone to go to the loo, or the whole tribe of us trying to find a big enough space at the front of the crowd. I wish I was old enough just to get on a train and go by myself.

There's a man I don't recognize hovering behind Auntie Jo. He's carrying a bottle of white wine and, instead of wearing shorts and a polo shirt like all the dads, he looks a little bit over-smart in his light pink shirt and linen trousers. Is this her new bloke, then? I stare at him and he smiles back awkwardly.

"Oh god," says Auntie Jo, clapping her hand over her mouth. "I'm so sorry, I got so excited about the marathon that I forgot my manners." She turns to the man. Then I spot that behind him, there's another man, this one holding a big bunch of flowers. So if this is Auntie Jo's boyfriend, who's *he*? Which one is it?

"This is my favourite nephew Aidan, and his best friend

Jack, who's kind of like an honorary nephew, aren't you, Jack?" She gestures at us both. "And this is Justin, my friend from work..."

"Nice to meet you, Aidan and Jack," says the first man, stepping forward. Jack grins and says hi, but I just nod. If he is Auntie Jo's boyfriend, I need to take my time to decide whether I'm going to like him or not.

"And this is Atif..." continues Auntie Jo, putting her hand on the other man's arm.

"Jo..." screeches Mum and, before she can finish the introductions, Jo's being squashed into a huge, overexcited hug. They all start exclaiming over how beautiful the flowers are and how lucky they've been with the weather and other boring stuff like that.

"Come on," says Jack. "I'm starving, let's get one of your dad's burgers."

I follow him in a bit of a dream, imagining myself crossing the marathon finish line together with Auntie Jo, being given my medal and wrapped in one of those foil sheets afterwards to keep warm. I've got the fastest time ever for a first-time runner. Mum and Dad are cheering and holding up signs by the side of the road, which say stuff like "Go Aidan" and "Team Taylor". Bells, Chloe, Daisy and Evie aren't in my dream, perhaps someone else is looking after them...

I turn round and catch a glimpse of Justin. His hand is resting on Atif's back. Atif turns to him and whispers something in his ear and they both laugh. There's something about how they look together. I can't stop staring. I mean, maybe I'm wrong. And they're not…but, are they?

Chapter Two

I'm distracted for the rest of the afternoon. I can't help it. I keep trying to glance over at Justin and Atif, without them – or anyone else – noticing me looking. It's not easy. So many people keep getting in my way. But I feel like if I let them out of my sight, even for a minute, I might miss something crucial. I'm just not sure what.

It must be obvious I've got something on my mind. Even Jack's impatient with me for not paying attention to what he's saying, and he can normally chat on for hours without needing much response from me.

"So, what do you think, Ade?" he asks, through a mouthful of burger. "Do you agree with me or with Bells? It's important."

Bells is only hanging out with us while she waits for her

best friend Lily to turn up. Lily's okay, but she's so loud. I don't mind that she's not here yet. Although, if Lily's coming, there's at least some chance Will, her brother, will come too. He's a couple of years above me and Jack, tall, curly-haired and kind of cool. Even though Lily's in and out of our house all the time, I've hardly ever spoken to him. I'm not sure he properly knows who I am.

"Er..." I say.

"You could at least *pretend* to listen."

"I was," I protest, even though I wasn't.

Atif's just sat down in a corner of the garden with Evie; it looks like she's showing him some of her toys. Justin's talking to Dad, and Dad's laughing. What are they talking about? Could it be about me, or is that just stupid? Jack's staring at me.

"So, who's right?" he asks again.

"You, Jack, you're right," I say at last.

"Why?" he asks, accusingly. "*Why* am I right?"

I sigh and force myself to focus on Jack. "Oh, all right, I give in, I *wasn't* listening. Whatever, I still reckon you're right. What does Bells know about anything?"

Bells sticks out her tongue at me. "Shut up, Aidan."

"We're talking about the set for the play," explains Jack, now he thinks he's got my attention. "Bells thinks it should be all silver and gold material and fairy lights—"

"Like everything's soaked in starlight!" she interrupts.

"But that's a bit tacky, you know, instead I think we should bring in loads of branches, flowers and stuff, make it really look like a real forest."

"Yeah, like I said, you're right. Anyway, you're the one in the play, not her. Bells isn't even old enough to be in it."

Jack's got one of the main parts in the school production of *A Midsummer Night's Dream* at the end of term. I hardly understood a word of it when we did the play in English last term, and what I did get – fairies and people falling in love with each other and running away from their parents – well, it seemed a bit silly. Why would anyone care what happened? All I properly remember is there's a character called "Bottom" and every single time he got mentioned, it made some of the boys snigger and Ms Ashby sigh and shake her head. But Jack's really good at acting, and he loves it. So because of him, I now know every detail of the play.

"Here, look," says Jack. "Look at your mum." He nods over at Mum, who's talking to Avni from next door. They're leaning over a pram, and then Mum reaches in and scoops up a tiny baby in a little white sunhat, cradling him in her arms with this dreamy look on her face. "Don't you think she looks a bit broody?"

"Don't even joke about it," I say. "No more babies.

No way. Four sisters is enough. You don't know what it's like."

"One brother's enough too," says Bells quickly. "Too much actually. Anyway, Mum's already given Avni most of our old baby stuff. She says there's no point in keeping it any more." She suddenly springs to her feet. "Oh look, Lily's here…laters!"

I watch as Bells makes her way across the garden. I'm checking if Lily's by herself or the rest of her family have come too. It's easy to spot Will. He's wearing a plain white T-shirt and jeans, but he looks great, older than fifteen, I reckon. I look away quickly in case he notices me staring and concentrate on what Jack's saying. Even though Will's here, he was probably dragged here by his parents. It's not like he'll be hanging out with us, is it? And if he did, what would I say to him?

"Would it be *that* bad if your mum had another baby?" continues Jack. "I mean, wouldn't you like a brother?"

"Nah, no point. By the time he'd be old enough to be any good, I'd have left home."

"Anyway," says Jack, grinning. "You don't need a brother, do you? Not when you've got me." He nudges my arm. "Come on, let's get some more to eat. Can't you hear those hot dogs calling my name?"

I'm just squirting the ketchup on my hot dog, when a

voice right behind me says "Hey, Aidan, you all right?" It makes me jump and I squeeze the bottle extra hard by mistake. The air in the bottle makes this loud farting noise and ketchup spurts out all over my hand and over the table.

I'm desperately looking for something to wipe it off with, when Will reaches over from behind me with a whole load of paper napkins.

"Er, thanks," I say, taking the napkins from him and dabbing at the mess everywhere. I don't look up. My face is probably as red as the ketchup.

"Didn't mean to give you a shock," he says. I can hear the smile in his voice. He's laughing at me. Of course he is, I've just made a total fool of myself. Although at least I didn't get any ketchup on my clothes, or Will's white T-shirt.

"You okay now, mate?" he asks.

"Yeah, yeah, thanks," I mumble, wishing I was a million miles away. But at the same time I don't want to go anywhere. I want Will to keep talking to me.

"What you got on there?" he asks, pointing at my plate.

"Oh," I look down at my hot dog as if I've never seen it before. "It's mustard, onions, gherkins, brown sauce, Dad's barbecue relish and...ketchup. Too much ketchup actually."

"Looks good," he says approvingly. He has this really nice smile; it's genuine, not like he's laughing at me after all. "You can't have too much ketchup I don't think." He takes the bottle from my hand and squeezes ketchup on his own hot dog. No mess. No embarrassing sound effects. "It's a good barbecue, this. I only came cos I couldn't face doing any more revision today. What year are you in, Nine?"

"Eight," I say, standing up a bit taller.

"Just you wait till *you're* doing GCSEs." He shakes his head. "I tell you, it's a nightmare. My mum's always on at me to do my revision, she hardly lets me out of her sight."

I nod, trying to think of something to say that makes me sound grown-up and like I understand.

"I told her I might audition for the school play," he continues before I say anything. "You know, I thought it might be a laugh, a couple of my mates are in it, but she went wild about it taking time away from studying. Not really my thing anyway."

"My best mate's in the play," I say. "He's got one of the main parts actually."

"Cool, well, maybe I'll see you there."

He picks up another paper plate piled with food from the table. "Anyway, I said I'd take this over to my mum. She's by the gate chatting to yours, I think. See you later."

"Yeah, see you."

I take a deep breath and run over in my mind what just happened. Will knows who I am. He called me "mate". He thinks I look like I'm in Year Nine. He said he'd see me at the play.

I'd better go and see where Jack's got to. I wonder if he'll want an extra hot dog. My throat's too dry to swallow mine now, and my stomach feels too jittery to eat any more.

By the time it's seven and Auntie Jo, Justin and Atif are getting ready to go, the garden's almost emptied out. Lily, Will and their parents left ages ago.

Auntie Jo leans in towards me while everyone else is saying goodbye. "Sorry, you and me didn't get to talk much today. I just felt I needed to keep an eye on Justin and Atif, make sure they were okay. I mean, they didn't know anyone else here. But your mum and dad are always so welcoming, I knew it would be fine. They've, well, they've had some bad news and I thought the barbecue might cheer them up a little."

"So," I say, my throat dry. It's a stupid question, but I have to be sure. "Justin's not your boyfriend then?"

"No," says Auntie Jo loudly, bursting out laughing. Mum looks up at her for a moment, and she lowers her voice. "No, sorry, Justin's a friend, a colleague from the

London office. We've got a meeting for the whole company on Monday, so I thought it would be nice for him and Atif to come and stay the weekend before." She looks at me. "What made you think he was my boyfriend?"

"Dunno," I say, staring at my feet. "I thought Mum said..."

"Of course," says Jo. "That's typical of my sister's wishful thinking. Justin's Atif's boyfriend, well, his husband actually. He's not my boyfriend. I thought you'd have worked that out."

"Yeah, well, of course, I know that," I mumble. As soon as she said "husband", I could feel my sticky-out Taylor ears going red.

I look away, hoping that Auntie Jo won't notice my awkwardness. I catch sight of Justin and Mum with their phones out. It looks like they're swapping numbers. But why?

"Exciting about the marathon, isn't it?" Auntie Jo says quickly.

"Yeah, it's amazing."

I'm so grateful that she's changed the subject. Auntie Jo's the opposite of Mum, she always knows when to stop asking questions or when not to say anything. Whereas there's no stopping Mum once she gets started.

"Run next Sunday, then? Just you and me? Only a short

one, I won't need to start training properly for ages. Just need to keep my base fitness up now. Thought I might do a couple of races, like a 10K, maybe a half marathon, in the autumn, to get into practice. What do you think?"

I nod, but before I can answer properly, she looks round and smiles at Justin and Atif, who are hovering by the gate from the garden.

"Oh, better go, the guys are waiting."

"Laura, Pete, lovely to meet you, thank you so much," says Justin. "What an amazing spread, especially those kebabs. I think I've eaten enough for a week." He's really sucking up, but Dad doesn't seem to notice, he just wipes his hands on his "Team Taylor" apron and beams. "And Laura, thanks for listening to me going on, I hope I didn't bore you too much with our problems."

"Not at all," says Mum, smiling. "Honestly. I hope it works out for you."

"Bye, Aidan," says Justin warmly. "Sorry we didn't really get a chance to speak properly, maybe next time?"

I don't say anything. Mum nudges me and hisses my name.

"He's just a bit shy," she says apologetically to Justin and glares at me.

"Oh, yeah, bye," I say, not meeting his eye.

My whole body is still tense, like I'm about to start

a race. As soon as they've gone, I feel like I can breathe normally again.

I've seen gay people before. Course I have. Loads of times. On TV. On the internet. In pictures from *Sheffield Pride* in the Star. I could probably write a list of every single time.

But never in my garden, chatting to my mum, eating my dad's barbecue, playing with my sisters. Not where they could see me, notice something I say or do or just the way I am, and know in an instant what I've told no one else, not even Jack or Mum or Auntie Jo – that I'm gay too.

At least, I think I am.

Justin and Atif seemed nice enough, but it's like just by being here, they've waved a great big spotlight around. Unless I'm very careful, that spotlight will fall on me. Then everyone will know and they'll all treat me different and nothing will be the same again. But I won't let that happen. I'm not ready for anyone to know. Especially not Will. Not yet. Maybe not ever.

I'm glad they've gone now. Auntie Jo said they lived in London, didn't she? That means I'll probably never see them again.

"Nice lads, weren't they?" says Mum to no one in particular once they've gone. "Really nice. I mean, look at those gorgeous flowers they brought. Really thoughtful."

"And the wine," says Dad approvingly. "That can't have been cheap. And they were vegetarian. I thought we'd done too many of those veggie kebabs, no one ever eats them, do they Aidan? It's not what you come to a barbecue for, is it, vegetables? But Justin must have nearly cleared me out." He shakes his head. "Shame they're not exactly boyfriend material for Jo though, she could have been on to a good thing with either of them."

"I thought they were a bit fake," I say. My voice comes out louder and whinier than I mean it to. "You know, showing off, with their fancy wine and flowers and everything. And I don't know why they came without even being invited. It's not like they're your friends or anything. That's just rude."

Mum turns to me. "For goodness' sake, Aidan. What's got into you? You've been off all day. Go and do something useful, there's plenty of clearing up needing doing. Go on." She waves me away. "Don't spoil things for everyone else."

I walk over to Jack, hands shoved deep into my pockets, and he looks at me, surprised. "What you said wasn't fair, Aidan," he says quietly.

He's right. But knowing that makes me feel even worse. Now I'm not just angry with Justin and Atif, and angry with Auntie Jo for bringing them to the barbecue in the first place, I'm angry with Mum and I'm angry with Jack, but most of all, I'm angry with myself. I should have kept my mouth shut.

There's only one thing I know that will make me feel better.

"Where do you think you're going?" shouts Dad after me, as I head back into the house.

"Getting my running stuff," I say without looking back. I know he's going to try and stop me.

"Let him go," I hear Mum say to Dad. "Whatever's up with him, he's better off out of here for a bit."

"Go on then," shouts Dad again. "But there'll be a pile of washing up waiting for you when you get back, all right?"

"All right," I say, putting all the bitterness and anger and wrongness I feel into those two words. "All right."

JUNE

Chapter Three

It's tipping down outside, but I'm already wet from swimming so it doesn't bother me that much. Even so, I wait under the bus shelter outside school till Jack's out of rehearsal, then we can walk home together.

"Has the 257 gone?" asks Ethan, running into the shelter with Sam close behind him. They're in 8H, same as Jack, but I only know them from swimming club. They're both faster in the pool than me, but I'm fitter, I can do more lengths without stopping than either of them. Easily.

"Dunno," I shrug. "I'm not waiting for the bus anyway, I'm waiting for Jack. We walk home together."

"What, Jack Ramscombe?" asks Sam, smirking as if I've said something funny. There's about five Jacks in Year Eight so it does get confusing. "Jack *Ramscombe*'s your mate?"

"Yeah, he's got rehearsal, they finish just after us. You know, *Midsummer Night's Dream.*"

"Oh yeah, I know, Jack's the fairy king, isn't he? I reckon he'd be really good at that," says Sam, but not in a nice way, not like he really thinks Jack's a good actor. Which he is. I'd think that even if I wasn't his friend, it's obvious. Ethan laughs. I clench my fists.

"It's a bit weird, isn't it?" continues Sam. "A lad wanting to get all dressed up as a fairy and everything, in front of everyone. I mean, unless he was..."

I step back quickly, as the 257 pulls in. It ploughs straight through a huge puddle and sprays Sam and Ethan with dirty water. Ethan swears loudly and they both climb on board without looking back at me.

But even seeing them get drenched isn't enough to make me feel better. I hate it when people say stuff like that about Jack. Okay, he doesn't know, but I still feel bad for him.

I can't help thinking it's his own fault sometimes though. Maybe if he just tried to fit in a bit more, people would leave him alone.

It's not like it's even the toughest lads who go to swimming club. It's not the football team or anything. Swimming's not cool at all, it's all people like me who hate team sports. Sam and Ethan aren't especially popular or anything like that. If even *they* feel it's okay to have a go at Jack – even if it is behind his back – perhaps I *should* warn him about what they're saying…

I peer out and see Jack walking up to the bus shelter. I shake my head – it's daft, he won't even run to get out of the rain.

"'*Therefore the moon, the governess of floods, pale in her anger, washes all the air*'," he says in a dramatic voice, smoothing down his wet, floppy hair. I hadn't noticed till now how long it's getting.

"What?"

"It's from the play," he says cheerfully, snapping out of his acting voice. "It means something like…'it's raining'. I think it does, anyway. Dunno really. Sounds good though. Rehearsal was wild today…"

"Oh yeah, go on." Jack's always full of stories and his stories always make me laugh.

"You know how India's the fairy queen, Titania, in the play?"

"Uh huh." India's a girl in my form. She's small and slight but has got this really grown-up voice. She sounds just like a queen should sound. It seems like solid casting to me.

"Well, that's her line, the one I said before about the moon washing the air. Except today, she got it wrong, so instead she said that the moon was washing her *hair.*"

I glance at Jack, waiting for more. So far, this isn't exactly his *best* story. He acknowledges my lack of excitement.

"Well, okay, it wasn't *that* funny, maybe you had to be there, but it gave India the giggles. And then once she started, it set everyone else off. A few of the Year Sevens start sniggering every time Titania gets mentioned anyway, cos it sounds rude, so they were halfway to hysterics already. Ms Ashby made us all do breathing exercises to calm down..." He pauses to mimic her taking deep breaths and letting them out with a slow whistle. "But that just made things *worse.* Have you ever tried doing breathing exercises while trying not to laugh?"

I shake my head.

"Well, basically it meant that there'd be about two seconds of silence, and this exploding noise as someone else tried, and failed, to keep their giggles in. Lewis in Year Nine – he's playing Puck – I swear he nearly wet himself."

"Oh right," I say. Any other time it would be funny, but I'm not feeling it today. I can't stop worrying about what Sam said earlier about Jack. Not just what he said, but what he meant to say. He was laughing at Jack because he seems a bit, well, gay. It doesn't matter if it's true or not, it just matters what it looks like.

I don't know if he is. He's never said anything to me. How would I feel if he was? Pleased, because then there's something else that we share, that binds us together? Afraid, because if he's gay and okay with it, then I've got no excuse to avoid working out what I feel about myself? Or worried, because if he's getting picked on now, then will it be me next? It's like when Atif and Justin were here, and it felt like there was this spotlight moving closer and closer, ready to focus on me.

We walk on for a bit. We're not saying anything, but so many thoughts are jostling with each other inside my head.

"What's up with you?" Jack asks.

"Nothing."

"Really? No offence, Aidan, but you seem in a right mood."

I shrug. "I'm okay." But then I think, perhaps now's a good chance to say something. If I can find the right words. "It sounds like it's great being in the play," I start. "And that's cool and everything. But, you know, I just wondered whether, I don't know, it might be a good idea to try and, well, fit in a bit more. In general, I mean."

Although even as I'm saying it, I can't imagine a world where Jack Ramscombe tries to fit in. He acts as if the whole world should fit in with him instead.

He looks confused. "But I *do* fit in. I fit in with everyone else in the cast. We all get on fine, it's a laugh."

"Yeah, but that's just the drama kids," I say. Right now, I'm not thinking about them. I'm thinking about the boys like Sam and Ethan who use the word "gay" when they really mean "rubbish", or the girls who giggle and whisper mean things about anyone who stands out. "I mean, they are, you know…" I tail off, not able to say what I mean. "What about everyone else? Can't you just, I don't know, tone it down a bit sometimes? Around school, when you're not onstage, I mean?"

"Tone it down," he says slowly. "Tone what down?"

Everything, I want to say. The way you look, and walk, and speak. I understand that's just how Jack is, but not everyone does. I only want to look out for him, make sure he's okay, like I've always done.

In the end I just say, "I dunno."

"Do you mean that I…embarrass you, Aidan?"

"No, you don't, course not, it's not that, it's… Oh, never mind," I say. "I'm just trying to help, that's all."

We've reached my house by now, and the rain's still pelting down. I can feel it trickling down my back and seeping through my school shoes. It's a bit much now, even for me. I want to get inside before I get even wetter, but I don't want to leave things feeling awkward. I think Jack feels the same. He takes his glasses off and wipes them on his sleeve.

"You done the French homework yet? Writing about your holidays?" he says.

I grimace. "Nah, got to do it tonight. Got no idea though, going to have to make something up."

"Me too. Message me if you get stuck, yeah? We can work it out together."

"Thanks." I grin at him. It's not just thanks for the offer of help, it's thanks for making it feel okay between us again, at least for now.

I let myself in. It feels so good to be out of the rain and in our nice, dry kitchen, even if it is full of people and there's no space to sit.

"Budge up, Bells," says Mum. "Let Aidan sit down. Here, I'll warm up your pizza in the microwave. It's cats and dogs out there."

"Thanks, Mum. I know, I've just been out in it."

"I suppose you have."

"So, Mum, *can* I make a cake for Sunday?" says Bells, ignoring me and continuing a conversation they obviously started before I came in. Chloe, Daisy and Evie have finished their tea already and are playing a noisy game of Top Trumps.

"That would be lovely," says Mum. "Try and use a proper recipe this time, not simply throwing in everything we have in the cupboard."

"I just like being creative, that's all," says Bells.

"What's happening on Sunday?" I ask. I flick through all the family birthdays in my head. No, I haven't missed anyone, and there's nothing marked on the family wall planner on the fridge – the one where Evie and Daisy have to share a column, as do Mum and Dad, because it's not big enough to fit in the whole of our family.

"You remember Justin and Atif?" says Mum. "Auntie Jo's friends?"

"Uh huh," I say, like I'm not really listening. Like I haven't been thinking about Justin and Atif every day since the barbecue. Wondering what it would be like to be gay and not mind everyone knowing, or to be grown up and have a boyfriend, or even a husband. And whether that could ever be someone like Will. Since seeing them at the barbecue, there's been a picture in my head that wasn't there before. There's a possibility. But it's too weird to think about for long.

I kind of wish I'd spoken to them properly, maybe I could have been a bit more friendly, when I had the chance. I wonder how old they were when they knew, really knew. Nearly thirteen like me? Older? Younger? And *how* did they know? But, even if I had spoken to them, I know I couldn't have asked them any of those things, so what would have been the point?

"They're coming to lunch on Sunday."

"What, *this* Sunday?" I burst out. "Like in five days' time?"

"Yes, this Sunday. Here's your pizza. And don't forget to hang your wet stuff up straight after you've eaten. I don't want to find it in a mouldy pile in your room in a week's time, okay?"

Every Tuesday, when I get back from swimming club, we go through the same routine, where Mum tells me the same things about hanging up my stuff. Sometimes I remember to do it, but usually I don't.

"But why? They were only here the other week. And you hardly even know them. And they live in London."

"We got on well," says Mum. "Anyway, it wasn't the other week, it's nearly a month since the barbecue. Which reminds me, I hope you'll be a bit more polite when you see them this time."

I grunt, pretending to concentrate on eating my pizza.

"Is it just them coming?" asks Evie, looking up from the game. "Haven't they got any kids for us to play with?"

I can't think of any of Mum and Dad's friends who *don't* have kids, except Auntie Jo of course, and Avni and Ramesh next door, but they've got their new baby now.

"Don't be silly, they're both boys. They can't have children," says Daisy firmly. "You need a mummy *and* a daddy to have babies. That's what Mum told us."

She looks up at Mum for confirmation, but Mum just sits there with a thoughtful look on her face.

"Course they could. You're the one who's silly. They could've adopted children, couldn't they?" says Chloe.

"Maybe..." Daisy still looks sceptical.

"I liked Atif best," says Evie.

"I bet you did," says Bells, swiping a couple of chips off my plate. "He listened for hours while you told him the names of all your soft toys and then tested him on them afterwards. No one else would sit through all of that."

"He was nice," says Evie again.

"I liked him too," says Daisy, not wanting to be left out. "And Justin. He was funny."

"Well, you won't be here when they come. So there. You and Daisy are at Jade's party," says Chloe. "It says it on the planner."

Mum suddenly snaps out of her dream and starts clearing plates off the table.

"I won't be here either. I've got a race on Sunday," I say.

"What?" says Mum.

"A race. I told you ages ago. I've got to be over at Bradwell by eleven and all."

"Seriously? Is it on the planner?"

I fumble around on the table for a pen, and then scrawl "Bradwell race" in my column for Sunday.

"Yeah, course it is," I say.

"Well, I can't take you," says Mum. "Neither can Dad. Justin and Atif'll be here at twelve. Can't you get someone else from the club to give you a lift? You should have let us know earlier."

"I *did* let you know," I insist. "It's you. You just don't listen. Jack's mum never forgets things like this, important things."

"Jack's mum doesn't have to remember 'important things' for five other people. Six, if you count your dad. Still, if you, Evie and Daisy aren't here for lunch, that does mean more space round the table," she muses. "And I'm sure Justin and Atif will still be here when you get back, so that's all right."

All right for whom? I wonder.

Chapter Four

My muscles are aching after training on Thursday, but I think I'm just about ready for Sunday's race at Bradwell.

I'm taking it easy on the sofa next to Bells when Mum sticks her head round the door.

"Do you two fancy taking the dog for a walk?" she asks. "It's a lovely evening."

"Mmm..." I say. "Maybe. In a minute." Meaning, no.

"I'll come with you," Mum continues.

"Why?" says Bells, leaning forward. "Don't you have stuff to do?"

"Not really," says Mum cheerily. "Nothing that's more important than spending some quality time with two of my favourite children. And my favourite dog, of course."

Normally Mum speeds round doing about a thousand

jobs a minute. She never sits still. Her finding someone else to walk the dog would usually be part of a grand plan to free up her time so that she can listen to Chloe's reading while fixing a broken drawer and doing her invoices.

Bells sighs and turns the TV off. She pokes me. "Come on, Lazy."

"But I just sat down!"

"Well, get up again, you're supposed to be the exercise freak in the family. Let's go and exercise."

"What? I've already been exercising all evening!"

Bells ignores me and raises her voice, "Mum, will I need a jumper?"

"Look out of the window, Bells, and work it out yourself," I tell her, just as Mum says, "Maybe just a light one."

As she shuts the door behind us, Mum says, "The Field?" and we head up the road together, us chatting, Toto straining ahead on her lead.

When Toto was a puppy, we each wrote down our suggestions for what she should be called. Dad put all of them into the woolly hat with the earflaps – which used to be mine, then Bells's and now Chloe's – shut his eyes and picked one out. Chloe's suggestion won. She had just watched *The Wizard of Oz* which is why, years later, we get funny looks in the park when we call out "Toto" and a huge golden retriever bounds towards us.

Once we get to the Field, Mum takes Toto off her lead and we all sit down on the big flat rock at the top. Toto runs round madly, sniffing everything and barking at squirrels.

"Isn't this beautiful?" says Mum dreamily, looking out at the city and hills beyond. "I wouldn't want to live anywhere else. So many happy memories."

She's kind of right, it is beautiful up here in the early evening sun. All the rain from earlier in the week has disappeared. But I'm also sure there are other beautiful places in the world and that life exists beyond Sheffield.

"So." Her tone changes, suddenly practical again. She smooths down her jeans with her hands. "I need to talk to you both about something. It might all sound a bit strange at first, okay, but stick with me – it's also really exciting. But the most important thing to remember is, this family, we're a team, aren't we? We help each other and we help other people, and there's nothing we can't talk about together. Right?" She grabs on to one of our hands each.

"Er...right," says Bells. "Mum, are you okay?"

Mum thinks it's always right to be honest about everything. Nothing sugar-coated. But I'm not sure it's *always* the best idea. Like when I asked if Father Christmas existed, and she said no, but we could still have fun pretending that he did. Then, when I told everyone else in Reception that Father Christmas wasn't real, loads of parents complained. It sounds stupid now, but back then it mattered. I wished Mum had let me go on thinking he was real, just like everyone else did.

"Yes, Bells, I'm okay. Here's the thing..." She takes a deep breath. She looks nervous. It's not like Mum to be nervous. I start to pay proper attention. She must have something big to say. "Justin and Atif want to start a family and I'd like to help them. I'd like to have a baby for them, to be what's called their surrogate. Do you both know what surrogacy is?"

"Whoa, whoa, whoa, what?" shouts Bells, jumping up. She startles a pigeon which has been quietly perched on a low branch, and it flies away. "You want to have *another* baby, and then just *give it away* to someone else?"

Now that she's got the words out, Mum doesn't look at all nervous any more. She's her usual down-to-earth, unflappable self again.

"Well, I suppose that's it really," she says. "But it wouldn't be 'giving it away', as it wouldn't be *my* baby to give. It would be Justin and Atif's. I'd just be looking after him or her for them till they're ready to be born. You know, like child-minding; I look after other people's children all the time, don't I?"

"Mum, be serious," says Bells. "This is different. You'd be pregnant. You'd have a baby. I mean...come on, it's not like child-minding."

"I know, sorry, but I *am* being serious. Honestly, it wouldn't be *my* baby."

"But it would be *our* brother or sister, wouldn't it?"

"Not legally. And not really either. The baby would grow up with Justin and Atif, not with us. It wouldn't *feel* like having a brother or sister, more like a cousin, I guess, or like it is with Jack, someone who's a really important part of our lives but not part of our immediate family. We'd spend time with Justin and Atif and the baby as he or she grows up – but they'd be a separate family."

"So, this baby, you won't be its mum then?" Bells continues the interrogation while I sit in silence. There's too much for me to take in for any words to come out. But Bells always has a million questions about everything – she was one of those little kids who drives you nuts asking "why?" – and this isn't any different. Mum's used to throwing answers back at her as fast as she can ask questions.

"Well, I will in a way, it'll be my egg. And Atif's sperm, in a syringe of course. All I need to do is insert the sperm into my body and..."

"Mum, stop it, TMI!" interrupts Bells, putting her hands over her ears.

"It's not TMI," insists Mum. "It's exactly the *right* amount of information. I've never seen the point in keeping anything from you kids, just because of your age, not if it's something you need to know. Anyway, no, I won't be the baby's mum, not in any way which matters."

"So, the baby won't have a mum at all?" I ask, finally finding some words.

"No, but it will have two loving parents," says Mum, and she looks straight at me, long and hard. I look away before she does. "That's all that matters to me. That's all that should matter to anyone."

"So, *that's* why they're coming on Sunday..." I say slowly.

"Yes, that's right. We've been phoning and messaging a lot in the last couple of weeks, but we need to talk face-to-face. We weren't sure whether to tell you now, or after they'd come and you'd had a chance to get to know each other, but I think it's best to have it all out in the open right from the start. We'll be seeing a fair bit of them if this all works out."

"So, what happened?" says Bells. "Did they just, like, message you and say 'will you have our baby?' I mean, that's well weird."

"No, no, of course not, I offered. It was *my* idea – they were pretty surprised actually. At the barbecue, Justin told me how much they wanted to become parents, how they'd been getting to know a woman who had offered to help them by getting pregnant for them. It was all looking good, but then she got ill and had to drop out. They were so disappointed. They didn't *ask* me. I don't think it even crossed their minds. But I felt for them, I kept wondering how I could help. And then I realized, I can. I can help."

This is typical Mum. There's something about her which makes random strangers want to tell her their life stories, and that makes her want to fix their problems.

"But, aren't you too old?"

"Bells," says Mum, giving her a little shove. "I'm only thirty-seven, that's not old. Really. Plenty of women have their first babies at thirty-seven, not their sixth. My body knows how to do this. And I want to help someone else have the same happiness that your dad and I have got in our lives from having you lot. It's that simple."

"Does Dad know?" breathes Bells.

"You daft lass, of course Dad knows. Would be pretty hard to keep it a secret, wouldn't it? We've talked it over. He agrees. Your dad's got a big heart. But we thought it best that he told the little ones while I told you. Seeing as you're both a bit older, we thought you might have more questions." She laughs. "And I was right. Any more you want to ask now – or shall we drag Toto away from these interesting smells and go home?"

I shake my head. No questions.

"Well, if you think of anything, anything at all, just ask. Any time. Okay?" She ruffles my hair. Then she flicks the ball thrower back one last time. I watch Toto haring after the tennis ball, running for no reason except pure joy. I wish I could run after her. I wish things were that simple for me too.

"Oh my god," whispers Bells to me, as we head back down the street. Mum's a little way behind, poo bag in hand, waiting as Toto squats by a lamp-post. "I've *got* to tell Lily. She'll love it. I mean, it's so weird."

"No," I say, without even stopping to think. "You can't tell *anyone*."

"Only Lily."

"Not even Lily."

Lily has the biggest mouth in the school, even bigger than Bells does.

"But it's cool, like something on TV. I bet you'll tell Jack."

"No," I say. "It's not cool, it's embarrassing. No one else's mum would do this. It's like she's, I don't know, *addicted* to having children. Isn't it enough to have all of us without having a baby for someone else too?"

"Well, *I* think it's cool," says Bells firmly.

"I don't care what you think, you still aren't to tell anyone. Okay?"

It's not so bad now cos Bells is still in Year Six, but in September she'll be at secondary school with me. Everyone will know she's my sister, so whatever she says will always come back to me.

"Can't make me!" And she starts running down the road. I overtake her easily, then wait at the front door for her to join me before going in.

"Please," I say quietly. "Don't tell anyone yet."

"Oh all right," she sighs. "But if Mum does get pregnant, people will know, won't they? And I bet Mum and Dad will tell their friends, you know what they're like."

I know what she's going to say next.

"Better out than in!" we chorus together, echoing one of Mum and Dad's favourite sayings. And then we both start laughing.

"Ade, why don't you like Justin and Atif?" asks Bells. "They seem okay. Is it cos they're gay?"

"No, don't be stupid, course not," I snap. "I just, well, I don't know. We hardly even know them, do we, and now Mum says she's going to have a baby for them. Do you even think it's okay for a kid to have two dads? I mean, really? I've never met anyone with two dads. What about when they're at school and kids ask about their mum, what would they say?"

Bells looks at me in disbelief, hands on hips. Sometimes she seems much older than eleven. More like a smaller version of Mum.

"Ade, Mum's not even pregnant yet – chill out!"

"Good point," I say, feeling more hopeful. "Mum might not get pregnant at all or they could all change their minds or something. Maybe it will never happen." Then a thought strikes me. "Hey, Bells, what if she does have the baby and they decide they don't want it after all?"

"Dunno, I guess, we'd have a new brother or sister, wouldn't we? If we do get to keep it, I hope it's a boy. Then you'd be the one to have to share your room this time."

Chapter Five

It's raining again by race day, but I know I'm fit and I'm used to running in worse. I could get a good result today. It's the second last one of the season, so if this race goes okay, I've got a real shot at the Under-13s club trophy.

I wait at the bottom of the road for Charlie's dad to pick me up, all my kit in a bag on my back. The back window of his battered old Ford Fiesta's covered with stickers from various races and the windscreen wipers at the front are zooming backwards and forwards as the rain pounds down.

"Mum or Dad not coming today, Aidan?" he asks as I squeeze in the back seat next to Charlie. "Never mind, you know I'm always happy to take you, you tell them that."

I learned quickly that, when you've got a big family,

extracurricular activities need to be cheap and easy to get to. At least fell running's cheap, and it's usually easy enough to cadge a lift.

Charlie's been running since he was tiny, both his mum and dad compete, and his dad's marshalling today. His high-vis jacket is slung over the passenger seat. Charlie's really quiet, but his dad's the total opposite, he's always talking, and has this huge laugh, but he never really remembers anything you say – unless it's about running. Then he's totally focused. Not like Mum or Dad, they still don't really get why I do it at all. Dad's pretty fit, you have to be if you're a firefighter, but he'd rather watch sport on TV than do it in his spare time. And Mum's always on the go, but organized exercise isn't really her thing.

"They're, er, busy," I say.

"Chasing round after you lot probably takes up most of their time, doesn't it? How many is it now?"

"Five."

"Five, my goodness." He laughs his booming laugh. "And twins! I don't know how you tell the difference between those little ones. Like two peas in a pod. Any of them show any interest in running yet?"

"Afraid not," I say, unable to imagine any of my sisters out on a course.

"Shame, shame, plenty of girls involved these days.

There's enough of you, you could have a Taylor sibling in every age category – I bet no family's ever done that before." He laughs again.

"My aunt's a runner," I say. "She's running the London Marathon next year. I'm going to be training with her, *and* I'll go to London and watch the race." For some reason, I really want to impress Charlie's dad.

"Is she now? That's pretty good. I ran London once myself, years ago, it's very flat though and… Oh, here we are." He turns sharply into the car park, where there are groups of runners in waterproofs standing round already looking drenched. "Lovely day for it," he proclaims as we make our way through the mud to join them. He's not even joking.

The race starts well. Uphill's always my favourite way to begin, I quickly take my place near the front. I like the way with fell running you can pick your own route, you don't have to follow everyone else exactly, so if you're clever it's easy to nip past someone and still keep at a speed you like.

I try to keep my mind focused, in time with my body, thinking only about the next few metres, where I next need to place my feet. But my thoughts keep wandering off track.

Right now, I think, Justin and Atif will be on their way

to our house, ready to hatch this crazy plan with Mum and Dad. A plan that could mean that they'll be part of all of our lives for ever. And no one apart from me seems to think it's crazy at all. I can't rely on a single one of my sisters to back me up on this. I'm sure that Bells thinks it's cool precisely *because* it's so crazy, Chloe hasn't said much but doesn't seem bothered, and both Daisy and Evie are already Justin and Atif's biggest fans.

I'm on a downhill slope now. It's steep and the rain's made it extra slippery. The mud's dark and gooey like chocolate fudge cake. I lose my footing, just for a second, and slide down faster than I intended. I catch my breath and then slow up a little just to be safe. Charlie runs past me, then a girl I don't know with a long ginger ponytail. I look behind me and there are a whole bunch of runners rounding the hill. Ahead, the leaders have already reached the bottom and are splashing through the stream. But I could still catch them if I put on a bit of speed.

Surely Auntie Jo can't think it's a good idea. But then Justin is her friend, so I guess she'd support him, whether or not she agreed with him. Although perhaps if I talked to her…

No, too embarrassing. I don't even want to think about it. I shake my head to try and refocus on the race.

I'm almost at the bottom when it happens.

It's like slow motion and top speed both at the same time.

I stumble, then feel my legs disappear under me. I fall forward, trying to steady myself with my hand, but I still hit the ground with a slam. It must have been a rock that tripped me. The mud and the slope mean I keep sliding after I fall. I can feel the stones grazing my knees and my elbows. I end up on all fours in the stream, the icy water making me shiver. A couple of runners stop briefly to see if I'm okay. I nod and wave them on without getting up. The rest can see Charlie's dad running towards me in his high-vis jacket and so keep passing me without pausing. There's no way I'm going to get a decent time or placing now.

Tears sting my eyes but I quickly blink them back before anyone sees. It doesn't matter, I tell myself, plenty of people trip and get back up again, they'll be another chance to get my time. At least I haven't twisted an ankle or anything like that. But none of it helps. It was my fault for getting distracted. All my fault.

"You all right, lad?" says Charlie's dad, pulling me to my feet. "All in one piece?"

"Yeah, I'm okay," I gasp, trying to brush some of the mud off my knees. "I'll keep going."

"If you're sure," he says doubtfully. "Make sure you get yourself checked out properly at the end."

I wave at him, and start hobbling my way round the rest of the course.

I feel better as I near the finish, even though I'm coming in with the newcomers and the younger kids. Running does that. Makes you feel better. Even when you're cold and wet and everything aches. It's all about you, on your own, pushing your body further than it wants to go. That's what Mum and Dad don't understand.

By the time I've finished a massive hot chocolate and an energy bar, been checked over by the first-aiders and Charlie's dad has organized all the marshals to collect in the course-markers, it's mid-afternoon and the rain has pretty much eased off.

Even in my spare, dry sweatshirt, I'm shivering and can't think of anything I want more than a hot shower. But as we leave the Peaks and start to drive through the streets of the city again and I can see we're getting closer to home, I wish I could put off arriving back for a bit longer. Maybe then Justin and Atif will have gone, and it will be us – Team Taylor – just like we always were.

I open the front door quietly, kicking off my trainers, then stepping neatly over the tangle of shoes in the hallway, trying to sneak upstairs before anyone notices I'm back.

I'm halfway up before, "Aidan!" comes Dad's voice from the sitting room. "Come in and say hello."

I retrace my steps, dump my bag on the floor and reluctantly push open the door.

Mum and Dad are sat on the sofa, with Bells perched on one arm, clutching one of those magazines that she loves, but hardly ever gets, which come with free lip gloss and stickers. Mum has her feet up on the coffee table. It's weird to see her sitting still and not running around getting stuff done. Atif and Justin are in the two comfy chairs, relaxing, with their shoes off and mugs of tea in their hands, like they belong here. Toto is curled up at Justin's feet and he's gently stroking her head. It's like I'm the visitor, not them.

Everyone turns to look at me.

"Hello," I say, as instructed, and then try to retreat again.

"Wow," says Atif, staring at the streaks of dirt on my kit. "Looks like you had quite a race. Your mum and dad were just telling us all about your running."

I hover, just inside the door, running my hands through my hair and picking out clumps of dried mud.

"Yeah, I s'pose so." I glance over at Mum and Dad. What else have they been saying about me?

"How did it go?" asks Dad, but he can already tell by my expression and by the state of me that it wasn't a good day.

I shrug.

"Never mind. There's always next time. I'm sure you did your best," chips in Mum. She puts her feet down, about to get up. "Do you want a cup of tea? There's some of Bells's cake here too. It's a bit unusual but..."

"It's really delicious," says Justin. "You'll have to give us the recipe." Bells beams.

"Nah, I'm good," I say. "I just want to get in the shower."

Mum leans back again into her seat. "Good idea, but then come back down, okay, sweetheart? We've been talking over some plans—"

"I think I've got some homework..." I interrupt quickly. "Yeah, definitely, Maths homework. For tomorrow." I can't think of anything more awkward or embarrassing than sitting round discussing my mum's plans to get pregnant. I mean, really.

"I'm sure it can wait," says Mum. "Or maybe one of the lads could give you a hand with it. Atif works in, what is it, insurance...?" Atif nods. "I bet you need a pretty good head for figures for that, right?"

"Well," says Atif, sensing my reluctance. "I'd be happy to have a go, but only if Aidan wants me to. I'm sure it's all changed since I was in school anyway, I don't know how much help I'd be."

"And there's no point in asking me," laughs Justin. "Sorry, anything with numbers just makes me switch off."

"Me too," says Mum.

"Don't listen to her," says Dad, turning to Justin. "She's the brains of this outfit. She's the one who runs her own business, does all the accounts and everything. She's got a much better head for numbers than I have."

"Ah, maybe," says Mum, squeezing Dad's hand. "We're a team."

Once I get upstairs, I wonder about hiding out in my bedroom and not coming back down. I bet that's what Chloe's doing. But I figure it's better to know what's going on than to be left guessing and worrying. And I've got an escape plan – Jack's just messaged me to ask if I want to go round to his later.

When I come downstairs, clean and changed, there's laughter coming from the sitting room, and I can hear Bells's high-pitched, overexcited voice telling one of her stories. When I push open the door again, I feel a bit like I'm interrupting the party, except that Mum has made me a cup of tea, even though I said I didn't want one, and she's moved up closer to Dad so that I can squeeze in next to her on the sofa.

"How long till Daisy and Evie are dropped back?" asks Dad, checking his phone.

"Not for a little while," Mum replies.

"Hey," says Justin, leaning forward. "Daisy and Evie, I've just got it. I'm right, aren't I? Daisy and Evie are the youngest. And before them, it's Aidan, Bells and...Chloe. They're alphabetical. I can't believe I didn't spot it before."

"Yes," says Dad, beaming. "We didn't start out with that as a plan, mind. Aidan was named after my granddad."

"And I'm Isabella really," says Bells. "But no one calls me that. There's, like, five Isabellas in Year Six. At least." No one corrects Bells's exaggeration.

"But it's a bit of fun and it does helps us remember who's who, keeps everyone straight. I mean," he says quickly. "Not straight, like, keeps them in order. Easy to remember, that's what I'm saying."

"And, you don't think you'd want another one? Sorry, that's a personal question, you don't have to..." Justin looks embarrassed.

"Look," says Dad. "If we're really going into this surrogacy business, there's going to be a heck of a lot more personal questions being asked round here, so we might as well all get used to them. You can ask us anything you like. Don't be shy about that. Just ask away. Better out than in. That's what we say to the kids too."

"Thanks," says Justin, sounding relieved and a look passes behind him and Atif. "We already feel so relaxed with you both. It's remarkable really."

"Us too," says Dad with a smile. "Now, as to having another one. Can't say we've not been tempted, but no. We're done. After all, I've got enough for a five-a-side team now, haven't I?"

Bells and I exchange looks. Dad loves calling us his five-a-side team, even though it's not like any of us play football.

"And anyway, got to stop somewhere. Certainly not going to get all the way to Z, are we?" He laughs again. Justin and Atif join in. Bells and I just grimace; we've heard all of Dad's jokes too many times already.

"Joking aside, Pete's right," says Mum. "We've no plans for more. And it's expensive having kids. You'll find that out soon enough, all being well."

She turns to me, adopting her "bright voice", the one she uses with the new children, the ones who look pale and unsure when their parents drop them off for their first time with a child-minder. "Now, listen to this, Ade, Justin and Atif have been telling us about these groups you can join, for families like ours, thinking about surrogacy, isn't that right?"

"Er, yes," says Atif. "There's meet-ups all over the place. At theme parks or playgrounds or cafés, that kind of thing. Both for women who are surrogates and their kids, like you, and for intended parents like us. It's just a chance to get to know other people on the same journey. It's been great for us. Really reassuring. You realize just how many other people there are in the same situation. You can ask questions. People are so generous with their experiences."

Playgrounds, I think. Like I want to spend my weekends hanging round kids' playgrounds with my little sisters, while Mum and Dad chat to a load of random strangers. *This is supposed to make me happier about the surrogacy plan?* If Mum's decided to do it, well, okay, but why do the rest of us have to get involved? I don't get how many of these families there can be anyway, when I've *never* met one before. And will all the people wanting kids be gay guys, like Justin and Atif? What would *that* be like? Just imagining it is exciting and terrifying both at once.

"Right," I say, keeping my voice flat. "Sounds great. Mum, is it okay if I go round to Jack's now?"

"What?" says Mum. "I thought you had homework."

"We'll do it together, and we'll take Toto for a walk if you like," I say. "I'll be back for tea."

"Oh, before you go," says Justin, half getting up. "We got you this."

He pulls a magazine out of his bag. It's the latest *Runners UK*, Auntie Jo usually gives me her old copies after she's read them. But this one's glossy and brand new. It's the best. Justin puts it down on the coffee table between us. I can't help but lean forward, straining to see what's on the cover, but I stop myself reaching over to take it. "I hope it's okay. We checked with Jo, she said you'd like it."

He looks straight at me, still smiling but unsure, like he's nervous, waiting for my reaction. Like a new kid at school who's trying really hard to get people to like him – maybe trying a bit too hard – but is secretly worried that they never will.

Atif puts his hand on Justin's arm. Every time they touch, so easily, so naturally, I want to look at Mum and Dad to see if they notice. And if they do notice, then what do they think? I mean, they *seem* okay with it. They must *be* okay because if not, why would Justin and Atif even be here, talking with them about having a baby? But would they be okay if it wasn't only Justin and Atif who were gay? If instead it was me?

"Yeah, thanks," I say, but I leave the magazine on the table, untouched. I don't want them to think it's that easy to win me over. I whistle, and Toto springs to her feet.

"Did you meet Jack at the barbecue?" Mum says as I'm leaving the room. "Aidan's best friend, like a second son to us really… You'll have to meet him properly soon…"

Bells jumps off the side of the sofa and follows us out.

"Can I come too?"

"What, to Jack's?" I pull on my coat. "No, find your own friends."

"Jack's my friend too."

"Yeah, whatever. You're not coming."

"I'll tell you all about what happened while you were out getting muddy."

"Like what?" I ask.

"Well, it's not just you that got a magazine, you know." She waves hers at me. "The twins got CBeebies ones, and Chloe got an art one."

"Wow," I say. "They really *do* want us to like them."

"Well, I like them anyway. They're nicer to me than you are."

"Oh shut up. I'm a brilliant big brother. The best."

"If I can't come to Jack's, can I go on the Xbox while you're out then?"

"Oh, all right," I sigh. "But don't touch anything else in my room, okay? What happened earlier then?"

She hops from one foot to the other. Bells is like Mum, you rarely ever see her standing still. "Nothing much really. They talked about expenses and medical check-ups and about signing an agreement to make sure the baby will be legally Justin and Atif's, I think. I wasn't really listening to that, it was pretty boring. Oh, and then loads about the team name. Dad got really into that."

"The what?"

"The team name. Justin said that when two families get together to try and have a baby, they call it a project and they usually come up with a team name. He sounded like he meant it as a joke, but Dad took it really seriously."

"A team name? What for? Dad's not thinking that we all put names in a hat like when we named Toto, is he?"

"Dunno, but I've got tons of ideas already. They're really good too. Justin and Atif really liked them. There's '*Team Unicorn*' or '*Team Dream*' – '*Team Rainbow*' is my favourite so far though, cos of all the different colours joining together and cos it's like the rainbow flags they have down at the park when it's Pride. Cool, right?" She looks at me, but I don't say anything. "I did what you said," she says quietly. "I haven't told Lily about it."

"Good," I say and shut the door behind me.

Whatever happens, I say to myself as I clip the lead onto Toto's collar, there is no way I'm joining Team Rainbow. Just like there's no way I'm telling anyone I'm gay. Absolutely no way.

JULY

Chapter Six

"What a perfect evening for it," says Mum, tucking the tickets into her handbag and shooing us out of the front door.

"It's not like we're going to be outside," I tell her. "We're just in the school hall. It doesn't matter whether the sun's shining or not."

She's right though, the sky's clear and the sun feels warm on my skin. It's a beautiful evening. Auntie Jo finished work early today and we went on a run before tea. I'm still feeling good after that. And I've been thinking about what Will said at the barbecue, that he might be coming along to watch his mates in the play. I hope I'll see him here.

"I *know* we'll be indoors," she says. "But it still feels all midsummery, doesn't it? Like something magic could happen. Even if it's just a night out for me for the first time in ages."

Me, her, Bells and Chloe are going to the play tonight. Jack's mum will meet us there. Evie and Daisy are too little to come, so they are staying behind with Auntie Jo. Dad's on shift.

"I don't mind missing it," he said to me in a whisper before he left last night. "Not really my sort of thing, you know, all that poetry and prancing about. You tell Jack 'good luck' from me though."

"So, explain to me again what it's all about," says Mum, as we walk down the hill. "I used to love English at school, but we never did this one."

I'm not really sure where to begin. "Okay, but honestly, it doesn't make any sense. There's this girl and she doesn't want to marry the bloke her father wants her to marry, but her best friend *does* want to marry him. And there's these fairies messing about in the woods with magic dust that makes people fall in love with each other, but usually the wrong people..."

"And there's the fairy queen, she falls in love with a donkey, Jack told me about her," adds in Bells.

"But at the end everyone marries who they're supposed to after all. Happy ever after."

"Well," says Mum, raising her eyebrows. "I suppose falling in love with the wrong person, or even a donkey, happens all the time, fairy dust or no fairy dust. But I do like a happy ending. I'm sure we'll follow what's going on, won't we, Chloe? The main thing is that we're here to support Jack."

Thinking about Jack makes me smile. He'll be so hyper right now, getting his costume on and going over his lines one last time, counting the minutes till it starts. All the same feelings that I get just before a race – nervous and excited and like I can't keep still. Knowing I can do it, but also like I have something to prove to everyone who's watching, worried in case it all goes wrong, like it did in Bradwell last month...

The sound of Mum's phone ringing snaps me back to reality. "Here, quick, take these," she says to me, tipping old tissues and receipts, a couple of pens and a packet of mints out of her handbag into my hands, as she rummages about for her phone inside it. "Where is the wretched thing?"

"Oh hi..." she says when she finds it. "Yes...yes... already? Traffic must have been amazing. I thought you'd be much later... Er... I don't know really... Jo's at the house, so you could just...hang on..."

Bells looks at me questioningly, but I shrug. I've no idea who it is either.

Mum moves the phone away from her mouth and turns to me. "Do you think they'll still have tickets on sale now?"

"Um, I guess."

"Great." She's back on the phone again, her voice animated. "Well, how's this? Do you fancy going to a play tonight? I know! We're just on our way to *A Midsummer Night's Dream* at Aidan's school. I mean, you don't have to. You can go and meet Jo if you'd rather..." There's a pause while the person on the other end says something, then Mum starts reeling off complicated directions to school, before telling whoever it is just to put it in their satnav and she'll see them soon.

"Who was that?" asks Bells. "Who's coming to the play?"

"It was Atif," says Mum.

"Atif? But Atif lives in London. What's he doing up here?" I say, confused.

I haven't seen Atif or Justin since the day of the Bradwell run, but Mum or Dad are always dropping their names into conversation, along with mentions of possible surrogacy group outings. If I try not to listen and don't respond to what they say, then maybe they'll stop talking about it and it will be like nothing's happening after all.

"Well," says Mum, smiling like I've said something funny. "If I'm going to get pregnant by using Atif's sperm—"

"Mum," I hiss. We're not that far from school now, anyone could be listening. "Be quiet." My ears are going red.

"*That's* not going to happen unless I see him every now and again, is it?" she continues, only slightly quieter. "He'll be coming up to Sheffield and staying with Jo every month until it works and I get pregnant. You know, Aidan, it's really good we're talking about this. If you have any questions, any time—"

"Okay, okay," I say quickly, trying to shut her up. I know Mum would love it if I did ask her loads of questions. She has all these books called things like *The Child Whisperer* or *Getting Teenagers to Talk* and I swear she studies them in bed at night, trying to find ways to get me to spill all my feelings out. But that's just not me.

"I get it. You could have said," I say.

"I did. You could have listened."

"It said 'Atif here' on the planner," says Chloe. I glare at her.

"You're not helping," I tell her.

I'm so shaken up that it's not until we get into the hall and sit down that I realize I'm still carrying all of Mum's junk. I shove it all back into her bag while she chats to Jack's mum.

Bells has found us seats right behind Lily and is leaning

forward, whispering and giggling, which means Will's in the seat right in front of mine. He's leaning back, relaxed, playing on his phone. At least if the play's boring, I think, I can stare at Will without him, or anyone, realizing. I'm glad no one can read my mind and they'll all be too distracted to notice if I'm blushing.

Mum's laid her cardigan over the empty seat between her and me, and I'm in the middle of sending a last good luck message to Jack, when she leaps up and waves her hands in the air.

"Atif!" she calls. "Over here. We've saved you a seat!" A few people turn their heads and stare, including Will. Mum's got a really loud voice.

Will sees me and smiles, that's all, but it's enough to make me go red. I pretend to look surprised to see him, like I haven't just been staring at the back of his neck.

"Not revising tonight?" I ask. It's the first thing that pops into my head.

He looks a bit confused. "Er, no, exams are over. At last."

"Oh," I say, feeling stupid. Of course they are, it's only a couple of weeks till the end of term. "I didn't mean that," I stutter. "I meant, how did the exams go?"

"Yeah, all right, we'll see. Just gonna enjoy my summer now."

Will turns back to face the front as Atif slides into the seat next to mine, whispering apologies to everyone else in the row who has had to stand up to let him through. Just then the lights go down and the curtains pull back to reveal the stage. It's decorated with branches, leaves and flowers, like Jack said it should be, but with fairy lights threaded through them, just like Bells wanted. They were both right. It looks amazing.

I know Jack's not in the first act. I can't really settle till I see him stride onstage at the start of the second. At first, I feel nervous for him – *I*'d hate it up in front of all these people – but I know *he*'s not nervous. He's loving it up there. Not only that, he's really good, at least as far as I can tell.

"Is that your friend?" whispers Atif, leaning over to me.

"Yeah, he's the one in green, with the crown. He's the king." Atif leans forward, watching the play intently. "I thought I recognized him from the barbecue; he wasn't looking quite so regal then though!"

When lights go back on for the interval, I blink in surprise. It feels like a spell's been broken. The play's so much less baffling now there's people acting it out, instead of just having to stumble through reading it in class.

"So," says Mum, turning to Atif. "What do you think so far?"

He smiles. "Yeah, it's pretty good. Justin will be sorry

to have missed it – he's more into this kind of thing than me. He's the arty one. Shame he had to work… Anyway, it's just nice to spend some more time with you and the family."

"Well," says Mum, patting him on the knee. "Better get used to it. This is your future. School plays, concerts, all of that. Fingers crossed anyway, eh?"

Atif smiles. "It's so hard to imagine. It feels like tempting fate to think too far into the future."

"It'll happen," says Mum. "It will. I'm sure of it. You deserve it, you two."

"I really hope so. You'd be invited too, to those school concerts, I mean. If you'd like to come…"

Mum's quiet for a moment. Her voice sounds a little bit wobbly when she says, "Yes, I'd like that. We all would, wouldn't we, Aidan?"

"Who's for a cuppa?" Jack's mum interrupts before I can answer. "I'm buying." She points over at a table with a huge urn where some Year Nines are filling paper cups of tea and coffee under Ms Ashby's supervision.

"Oh, Kelly, love," says Mum, in her normal voice again. "Your Jack, isn't he good? Such a natural up there. We're all so proud of him."

Jack's mum doesn't say anything, but she looks pleased.

"I'm not surprised though. He was always putting on

his own shows and things, wasn't he, when he was little? Now, yes please to tea. Two sugars for me. No, wait up, I'll come with, help you carry them all."

Atif says a polite no thank you to the offer of a drink. Good choice – the school tea is always disgusting, sort of scummy on top.

Everyone's milling around chatting now. Will's disappeared from the seat in front. I stretch up as tall as I can to see where he might have gone. He's across the room, talking to some other Year Elevens. I don't recognize them, except for Jen Thomas. She's a prefect and one of those girls that everyone says is really pretty – long, straight hair and lip gloss and perfect skin. One of the popular ones.

Lily kneels on her chair and leans over the back to whisper to Bells. I can't hear anything they're saying, just lots of giggling.

"Hey, Aidan, do you want a sweet?" asks Lily, staring at me and then looking away.

"Sure," I shrug. "What have you got?"

She produces a crumpled bag of Minstrels out of her pocket.

"Thanks," I say, digging my hand in. "My favourite."

"Are they?" she asks eagerly, like this is the most interesting thing she's heard all week, like she's storing the information up for… I don't know what. "Your favourites,

I mean, are they really?"

"Er…yeah, I s'pose so," I say and shake my head, not sure why this is so exciting for her.

Lily used to be okay to hang around with, but recently she's gone all weird. Now, anything I say seems to set her off giggling, even if it's not funny. If I answer the door when she comes round to see Bells, she just stands there staring at me, then when I try to leave, asks me loads of strange questions. I should ask Bells if she knows what's up with her, but I'm not really that bothered.

"Aidan, why aren't you in the play?" asks Lily, staring at me again.

"Me?" I say, surprised. "You're joking. No way would you get me up there."

"We're going to be in next year's play when we're in Year Seven, aren't we?" adds Bells, helping herself to a handful of Minstrels. "Jack says you have to audition, but that they always choose a play with loads of parts, so even if we're just in the background, we'd still be in it."

"Hmm," I say. Bells has never been an "in-the-background" sort of person; I can only imagine her in a starring role. I look round to see if I can spot where Will might have got to, but catch Atif's eye instead. He's looking at his phone, but I can tell he's really listening to us. He has this annoying, amused little smile.

"I s'pose you wouldn't have time to be in the play, not with your running," continues Lily, ignoring Bells. "We thought we might come and watch one of your races one weekend, didn't we, Bells?"

Bells and I both stare at her.

"Did we?" asks Bells loudly.

"Yes," hisses Lily. "Remember?" Bells looks blank. "We thought it might be fun..." Lily tails off, blushing.

I shrug. "I mean, you can if you like. It's normally pretty cold. And wet. And muddy."

"Here we are," says Mum, brightly, pushing her way past me back into her seat. "What a scrum. You'd think there was a national tea shortage or something. Just in time though, I think it's starting..."

Will slips back into his seat. Lily turns round, shooting me one last look. Atif puts his phone back in his pocket.

"Your sister's friend?" he says quietly to me.

"Yeah?"

Then he looks at me, as if not sure whether to say anything after all.

"I think she likes you. You know that, right?"

The music starts. The lights go down. I stare hard at the stage, waiting for Jack to appear.

I'm glad the second half's begun so I don't have to say anything in reply. Lily likes me. She *likes* me. It's so obvious that even someone who barely knows us can see it. And instead of me liking her, I fancy her brother. That's all messed up. This is the sort of thing that should happen in *A Midsummer Night's Dream* not in my real life. This is absolutely the last thing I need.

SEPTEMBER

Chapter Seven

It's the same every September. All-you-can-eat Chinese buffet. The day before term starts. Another of those Team Taylor traditions that Dad loves so much.

Last year, Mum suggested that perhaps we could go somewhere else, like the Harvester. Just for a change. The rest of us stared at her, and then we went to Wok Around the Clock as usual. All-you-can-eat is something we take literally. I'm already dreaming about piles of sticky ribs and crispy sesame toast.

"Come on, Aidan," calls Mum up the stairs. "The rest of us are ready, even Bells."

"Hey, what do you mean, *even* me?" says Bells indignantly. "I'm *always* ready in time. Mrs Hirst said I was one of the most organized people in 6H."

"Aidan, I swear you spend longer in that bathroom every day," continues Mum, ignoring Bells. "What are you doing in there?"

"Just coming!" I shout back.

I grab a clean hoodie off the clothes drier and wriggle it over my head. It's a bit short round my arms now, but it's still my favourite, so I tug the sleeves down to try and cover my wrists. Last day of freedom, when I can wear whatever I like instead of stiff, scratchy school uniform. I shove my hands deep into the pockets. Last time I was wearing this, I picked up a flier for some youth theatre thing that's on at the Lyceum cos I thought Jack might be interested in it. I meant to give it to him but I kept forgetting. It's not here any more.

I open the door just enough to stick my head out and shout down the stairs again. "Mum, Dad, who did the washing? Who took the stuff out of my pockets?"

"Guilty," says Dad. "Sorry, if there was anything, I probably chucked it."

"Good," says Mum. "You know I hate it when bits from old tissues get all over the clean clothes. Aren't you ready yet?"

I sigh. I don't really fancy going through the bins looking for the flier, but I'll have a very quick poke around, just in case.

I flip open the bathroom bin with my foot. No sign of the flier, just a load of old tissues – yuk, a used-up toothpaste tube, a couple of empty salt-and-vinegar crisp packets and a bit of white plastic poking out from right at the bottom. It doesn't look like rubbish, more like the end of a toothbrush, or one of those Covid lateral flow tests, or something that's been dropped in there by mistake. I pull it out. And then quickly drop it in surprise. It's not a toothbrush. Or a Covid test. I know what it is.

Downstairs, there's a shelf of scrapbooks that Mum's made. We've each got our own one, except Evie and Daisy who have one between them. Mine's got the most stuff in. I think Mum ran out of energy by the time she got to the others. They've got our baby photos, hospital wristbands, scribbled drawings, and pictures from the first day of school. The twins and Chloe still love looking through theirs and getting Mum to tell them stories of when they were babies. In there are all of our fuzzy, black and white, ultrasound pictures too – a record from before we were even born. And, in each scrapbook, the first page, even before the ultrasound picture, this: a photo of a positive pregnancy test.

I look again at the test I've pulled out of the bin. There are two blue lines across the little window in the middle. What does that mean? I try and remember what the pictures in the scrapbooks look like. Does that mean Mum's pregnant? Or does it mean the opposite? I'm just not sure and there's no time before we have to go out to check the scrapbooks downstairs.

But if she *is*, wouldn't she have told us? I mean, over-sharing is Mum's default setting, usually we can't shut her up. And this isn't just anything. It's important. It's going to change everything.

I try to push the thought to the back of my mind for now and focus on crispy duck and pancakes instead. My stomach's rumbling already.

I'll think about this tomorrow, not now. Or better still, pretend I never even found the test. I've done okay all summer holidays at not thinking too much. Even when Justin and Atif have been up, staying at Auntie Jo's. Even when everyone, except me, agreed with Bells that we should call ourselves Team Rainbow. Even when Mum and Dad tried to persuade me to go to one of those meet-ups for families exploring surrogacy. I told myself that I wouldn't normally hang out with Mum and Dad's friends – so why should this be any different?

Except that it is.

"At last," says Dad, as I gallop down the stairs two at a time and land with a jump at the bottom. But he sounds in a good mood, not cross with me taking so long.

"You haven't grown again?" says Mum. "That hoodie's already too small, look. I just hope your school uniform's still going to fit."

I look at Mum and Dad waiting with all my sisters by the door, jostling and giggling and excited. The people I know best in the whole world. Even Toto's there, always hopeful that someone's going to take her for a walk.

It strikes me all of a sudden. Mum wouldn't have thrown that pregnancy test away without taking a photo first, like she did for all of us. But that photo will never be in a scrapbook on our shelf. Because this baby won't have one of Mum's scrapbooks, they won't be part of Team Taylor, they won't have ears that look like Dad's, and they won't mess with my things or wind me up or finish all the cake because they won't be here. Instead they'll live in London with Justin and Atif. *Their* baby. It's not that I *want* another sibling, it's enough with the sisters I've got. It's just, I don't know, now that there *could* be a real baby, it feels weird and wrong that this baby won't be ours.

In an hour or so, we're sitting round the big circular table at the back of the restaurant, plates emptied and the white tablecloth sticky with splashes of bright sweet and sour sauce, eating ice-cream out of little metal bowls. It's still early in the evening but Daisy looks tired – she's climbed into Mum's lap and is leaning against her shoulder.

Next to her, Evie's wide awake and working her way steadily through the dot-to-dot book that she's brought with her. Dad's eaten loads, even more than me, and is leaning back in his chair, stroking his stomach in a satisfied way.

"Right," says Mum. "Time for this year's wishes. Who's going first?"

"Me!" says Bells quickly. "I've got mine ready."

Bells always loves to go first. Even though I knew it was coming – every year we each say our wish for the year ahead, it's part of the tradition – I need a little more time to think. We call them wishes, but it's more definite than a wish, it's something each of us is determined to make happen if we can.

"Go on then, Bells," says Mum, smiling. "What's your going-into-Year-Seven wish?"

"I wish I could be in a play, a proper one, like Jack's. Not like the rubbish little Year Six one, but on the big stage with all the lights and decent costumes and everything."

"That's a good wish," says Chloe. "Jack's play was really cool."

"Seconded," says Mum. "I think you'd be great, Bells. A natural."

"The audience would certainly hear you up onstage,"

says Dad, pretending to wince and cover his ears. "You've got a loud enough voice – you'd fill that whole hall and some. Isn't that right, Ade?"

"Er, yeah," I say.

I know Dad's just trying to get me to join in the conversation, but I'm too distracted. I keep glancing over at Mum. Does she *look* pregnant? She certainly doesn't seem any bigger than normal; she's in her same jeans and everything. When she was pregnant with the twins, she was enormous, I remember that, but I guess that wasn't until much later. How big would the baby be now? I try to remember from learning about it at school – the size of a grape? Or a lemon? Some kind of fruit anyway.

"Hey," says Bells, pretending to be annoyed. "I've got good voice projection, that's what Mrs Hirst says."

"I'm only joking you," says Dad. "It's a great wish." He lifts his beer in the air. "Here's to our Bells, future star of stage and screen." She beams.

"Better be you next, Daze," says Mum, shifting Daisy round on her lap. "Before you fall asleep."

"My wish is that I get picked to be the first one to take Mr Ted home and to write in his book," says Daisy firmly.

"Who's Mr Ted?" asks Bells. "And why's he coming to our house? That's a weird wish, Daisy."

"No, it isn't," says Mum. "You must remember, Bells,

Mr Ted's that teddy bear that lives in the Year Two classroom."

Bells makes a dismissive sort of noise. She thinks she's far too grown up now to have ever been as little as Daisy and Evie, but I bet she does remember. Mr Ted was around even when I was in primary school. He must be really tatty and old by now.

"Everyone takes it in turns to bring him home and to write a diary with him," continues Mum. "He's already been to our house three times, so I'm sure he'll be pleased to be back. Good wish, Daisy. What about you, Chloe?"

"I wish we could teach Toto some tricks. Good ones. So she could compete in a dog show," says Chloe. Mum and Dad look surprised, but I remember seeing things like *Dog Training for Beginners* and *Learn your Dog's IQ* on Chloe's most recent pile of library books.

Then Dad and Evie do their wishes. I'm not really listening, because all the possible things I *could* wish for, but could never say, are whirring through my head – I wish people would stop picking on Jack, I wish no one would find out I'm gay (*if* I am, I mean), I wish Will was interested in me – and Lily wasn't, I wish Justin and Atif would go back to London and we'd never see them again. I wish…

"You're a bit quiet tonight, Ade," says Mum. "Go on, your go next."

"What about you?" I ask.

"It's okay," says Mum softly. "I'll go last. Go on."

Then I realize. I bet she's waiting till now, for this moment when we're all together, to tell us about the pregnancy test.

But worrying about it won't stop her sharing, and I've thought of the perfect wish.

"I wish that we would all go and watch Auntie Jo in the London marathon. And that she'd do it in under four hours."

"Oh yes," says Bells, excitedly. "We are going to go, aren't we, Mum? Aren't we?"

"We'll see," says Mum. "But I hope so, I do want to be there to support Jo. Even if I think she's crazy. I mean, 26 miles."

"26.2 actually," I correct her.

"Yeah, that 0.2 makes all the difference! Nothing more for yourself though?"

I shake my head. Although if I *could* think of something to add, that might stop Mum saying whatever it is she has to say, just for a few more seconds. If she doesn't say it, then I can carry on pretending that I've got it wrong and she's not pregnant after all.

"Well," says Mum, fiddling with her ice-cream spoon.

She and Dad exchange a glance. I hold my breath.

"I'm sure you can all guess my wish for this year – that I can help Justin and Atif have a healthy, happy baby." She looks round at all of us. I know what she's going to say. I squeeze my hands together nervously under the table. "And...I've got a bit of news on that score. I'm, well, I'm..."

"Your mum's pregnant!" says Dad, proudly, not waiting for her to finish. "Isn't that brilliant?"

Bells shrieks and leaps out of her seat, knocking over her glass as she rushes over to hug Mum, and squashes Daisy, who's still curled up on Mum's lap. Evie takes this as her cue to leap on top of Mum as well. Chloe and Dad haven't moved but they are both smiling. Dad puts his arm around the back of Mum's chair. Bells's Coke is dripping all over the table, but no one else seems to have noticed. I don't say anything, just slouch down lower in my seat. I'm sure everyone in the restaurant must be staring at us now. I look round, hoping there's no one in here who actually knows us.

There's a couple over by the door, who look up from ordering their drinks to see what the noise is. With a sinking feeling, I realize I do know them. It takes a second to work it out. I'm not sure I've ever seen Charlie's mum and dad in normal clothes before, not running stuff. Maybe they haven't realized it's us. I look away quickly and duck my head down.

"Did you tell Justin and Atif yet?" asks Chloe.

"When's the baby due?" asks Bells at exactly the same moment.

"Hold on," says Mum. "One at a time. And, Evie, stop prodding my tummy, there's no bump yet. Yes, of course we've told Justin and Atif. They're really excited. They wanted to come up straight away, but they couldn't get off work, so they'll be here at the weekend to celebrate. And the baby's due, let's see, round about May, I reckon."

I feel like everything's closing in on me, like it's all happening too fast. There are so many thoughts rushing round in my head, that I don't even know what I think. What will I say when people start to notice that Mum's pregnant?

I push back my chair and stand up. I need to get away, just for a minute. I need some space.

"Just going to the loo," I mutter.

They're all talking so much that, for a moment, no one notices me. Which suits me fine.

"You all right, Ade?" says Dad, looking up. "You've gone a bit pale."

"Nothing, I'm fine," I say.

"You sure?" he asks.

Suddenly they all stop talking and stare at me.

"You don't *look* fine," says Bells.

"Shut up," I say. "No one asked you."

"Be nice to your sister," says Mum automatically.

"Look, I'm just going to the loo. By myself," I add, as Dad seems to be getting up too. "That *is* allowed, isn't it?" The people at the next tables have gone quiet. They are darting glances at us – this big, weird, noisy family – and then pretending not to. Then I realize it's just me they're looking at. I'm talking much louder than I meant to.

In the bathroom, I look at myself in the cracked mirror. My face looks flushed and upset. I run cold water over my hands and splash it on my face. It's just good to be by myself, no one around, no one hassling me. I wonder how long I can hide out in here.

When I finally push open the door back into the main restaurant, I look over at our table. Everyone's sitting around chatting and laughing. I slip back into my chair, take a deep breath and try to join in.

"Congratulations," I say to Mum, because I know that's what she wants to hear, and also because I can see how happy she looks. But it comes out sounding like I don't really mean it. Mum smiles at me anyway and gives me a sideways hug.

"Sorry if we're being embarrassing," she says quietly, just to me. "I know this is all a bit strange, and I know you're not sure about it." Not sure, I think, yeah, that's one way of putting it. I guess I haven't exactly tried to hide what I think. "But how often in your life do you get to help someone like this? Really help them, I mean. Change their lives for ever? I know you're a good lad, Aidan, I know you'd always want to help someone if you could, wouldn't you? That's all this is. Nothing more. But you might feel better if you talk about how you're feeling."

I pull away. That's her answer to everything. Talk about it. But what if I don't *want* to talk to Mum about this?

"Not us," she says quickly, seeing my face. "I don't mean us. Unless you want to. I meant, well, what about talking to Jack? That's what best mates are for."

"Maybe," I shrug.

"Just think about it, okay?" she says, turning back to the table. "All right, let's get the bill. Big news tonight, big day tomorrow and it's getting late. Evie, Daisy, do you need a wee before we go? Come on." She takes one of their hands in each of hers, and threads through the tables towards the loos, calling back, "Chloe, is that your jumper under the table? Don't forget it, love."

"Pete," booms a man's voice behind us, as Dad is getting out his card to pay the bill. "How's it going? Not got your fire engine parked outside today?" His laugh is nearly as loud as Dad's. He puts a hand briefly on my shoulder. "You all right, Aidan? All set for Sunday's race?"

Dad gets to his feet, grinning. He loves bumping into people unexpectedly like this, prides himself on always remembering a face and a name.

"Off duty tonight, mate. Although if you need any advice on getting a smoke alarm fitted, you know where to come." He laughs. "It's been a while since we've seen you. Laura and I must get down to one of Aidan's races again soon, it's just, you know, with all of this lot..." He waves a hand casually at our table.

"Of course," says Charlie's dad warmly. "You should try and make it though. Aidan's doing really well this season," he continues, like I'm not even here. "One tricky race, bit of bad luck, but otherwise, really impressive form." I can't help feeling pleased that he's noticed.

"Good to hear it," says Dad. "So, are you out for a special occasion?"

"Not really. Charlie's staying over at a friend's house, so we thought we might as well take the chance to have a meal out – just the two of us. But it looks like *you've* been celebrating something...?"

"You're right there. We have," says Dad jubilantly.

Please don't say anything, I think silently to myself, please. Just talk about the start of term or the weather or something. Come on, you can do it. But no, not Dad. Not now, not ever.

"I'll let you into the secret." Dad leans forward. "My wife's pregnant!"

"Congratulations," says Charlie's dad quickly, looking surprised. I can see him doing the maths in his head and coming up with the number six.

Okay, at least he's not telling them the whole story, about Justin and Atif and the surrogacy agreement.

"I'll tell you another thing." Dad pauses.

Oh my god, I think, maybe he is. Right here in the restaurant, in front of everyone.

"The best part is…it's not mine."

There's a moment of silence. Then Dad starts laughing, like it's a joke. It's obvious that Charlie's dad isn't sure whether to join in or not. It's so awkward. Even Bells is looking embarrassed, and nothing normally fazes her; not even the time when Mum and Dad dressed up as Superman and Wonder Woman for the fire station fancy dress party.

Surely Dad didn't *mean* to make it sound like Mum was having an affair. He can't just leave it there. He's going to *have* to explain everything now. I suppose it is good that Dad's comfortable being so open about everything, but he doesn't realize that not everyone feels the same.

"It's a long story," says Dad, wiping his eyes. "Not what you think though, I can guarantee it. I'll buy you a pint sometime and tell you all about it then. Or maybe at this lad's next race, eh?" He smiles down at me. I keep my eyes fixed on the Coke stain on the tablecloth, like I'm trying to read my future in it.

"Yes, absolutely," says Charlie's dad, who seems to be recovering. "Look forward to seeing you there." He hurries back to his table.

Just when I thought my parents couldn't be any more embarrassing. Is this what it's going to be like till the baby's born?

JANUARY

Chapter Eight

Jack and I are sitting side by side on my floor, our backs against my bed. His long, skinny legs are curled up in front of him, and he's still clutching his controller. It must have been getting dark outside all the time we were playing, but I've only just noticed. Most of the light in my bedroom is coming from the glow of the screen.

"Yes!" I shout, throwing down my controller in triumph.

I'm much more competitive than Jack, which means that I usually beat him. Even so, winning always gives me a buzz. It's tons better playing with him than with Bells – she normally loses interest and starts talking about something else at a crucial moment. "Another game?"

"Maybe in a minute." He yawns, stretches and checks

his phone. "Mum," he says, tossing it back on the floor without replying. "On about homework."

I've been so absorbed in the game that it's only now that I remember what I promised myself this morning. I've been putting it off for months, but today is the day I'm going to talk to Jack about Mum being pregnant, Justin and Atif, the surrogacy, everything.

Well, not quite everything. Not about how I feel about boys, or anything like that. Not yet. Not till I'm sure. And even then…

I'm going to talk to Jack, not just because Mum keeps going on about how I should. It's because I have to. It's getting pretty obvious; you just have to look at Mum to guess. Jack's here so much of the time that he'll definitely notice soon, or he'll walk in on a conversation about it in our kitchen, or my mum will say something to his mum. That's how Mum is. She doesn't like secrets. Especially not with Jack. Then it will be even more awkward if I haven't said anything. That's what I promised myself this morning. But now I'm wondering whether it wouldn't be better to wait till Jack finds out some other way. It's less of a big deal then, isn't it?

Jack sighs, picking up his phone again. "Oh, I'd better go back. I've got tons to do. Mum's really on my case – I hardly did anything last week cos of the auditions."

"Do you know yet if you've got it?" After everyone saying how good he was in *Midsummer Night's Dream*, and he really was, Jack wants to be Edmund in *The Lion, the Witch and the Wardrobe*. Bells is desperate to be Lucy, but I think cos she's only Year Seven, she'll end up being Second Faun or a lamppost or something.

Jack gives me a withering look. At least, I think it's a withering look, the light's too dim to see his expression clearly. "No, course not. Like I wouldn't have told you as soon as I heard."

"Go on," I say. "Stay just a bit longer. Tell your mum we're doing research for homework or something."

It'll be easier to tell him, I think, while we're playing. While we're both looking at the screen not at each other.

"All right then," he says. "It's only English, it's easy, I can always do it later." As Jack reaches for his phone to text his mum back, I notice something weird about his hands.

"Hey, what's that?" I ask.

"What?"

"On your nails?"

Jack stares at his hands for a moment, then spreads out his fingers to show me. "Ade, you are like the least observant person in the world, right? It's obvious. It's nail varnish. Bells lent it me. What do you think?"

"Er..." I'm not sure what to say. Boys don't wear nail varnish. At least boys at our school don't. "Are you a goth or something?"

"No, stupid. If I was a goth, I'd be wearing black, wouldn't I? This isn't exactly a very goth shade." True, it's a kind of light blue. It looks like it's from the set that Bells got for her birthday. "I just thought it would be fun, you know, to try. It doesn't mean anything."

It did kind of suit him, I guess. Would I ever want to wear make-up like that? Just the thought of painting something on me, even if it was just my nails, makes me feel itchy and sticky. I even used to hate getting my face painted when I was little. There's a photo in my scrapbook downstairs, of me aged about five, scowling at the camera, with a Spider-Man mask painted over my face. I still remember the feeling of wanting to wipe it off. Bells is next to me in the picture, beaming, with painted butterflies all over hers.

"Yeah," I say uncertainly. "I guess it looks okay, but you'll have to take it off for school tomorrow. It's against the rules." There's supposed to be a really strict no make-up rule at school, even though there are some girls in our year who always seem to get away with breaking it.

"No, you'd never dream of breaking the rules, would you, Aidan Taylor?" he says, but in a jokey way. And he's right. I wouldn't. "I s'pose I'll have to take it off. Shame though. I think it looks kind of cool, like I could be in a band or something."

I can't imagine everyone at school will think it's cool. Especially not boys like Sam or Ethan. They'll think something quite different.

"You wouldn't *want* to wear it for school anyway, would you?" I say. "I mean, people might say stuff."

"Seriously? Who cares what those small-minded idiots think?" he snaps. "What do they know about anything? The sooner I get away from that school, the better."

His voice doesn't sound like Jack's any more, he's normally so positive and funny about everything. Now he just sounds bitter and angry and I don't know why. I don't like it. It makes me feel worried. Jack and I have known each other for so long. I'm so used to knowing everything he's thinking, and him knowing everything about me. But I guess that's not true any more. Not for either of us.

"Hey, are you all right?" I ask. Has someone already been having a go at him, I wonder, just like I feared they would. "Has something happened at school? You sound..."

"Yeah, I'm fine," he interrupts. I don't think he is fine, he's just saying it to stop me asking any more, like I do when Mum asks me about how I'm feeling. But it's okay if he doesn't want to tell me. If it's something bad, maybe it's better not to say anything.

Then, all of a sudden, his tone shifts again, and he's back to normal, funny, messing-about Jack. "So am I finally going to get a win or not? Hope you're ready to lose this time, Ade. I'm gonna crush you."

"Yeah, sure you are, not with your rubbish tactics," I say, grinning back at him, as the home screen loads and the intro music plays. "Ready?"

I still haven't told him. Maybe now?

But the words don't come.

"Come on, let's play," I say, fiddling with the controls.

I'm trying to concentrate on the game, but my mind keeps drifting. I'm too busy trying to find the right words to say to focus on anything else. After a few minutes, but that feel like ages, I can't hold it in any more, I just blurt it out.

"Mum's pregnant."

I keep my eyes fixed on the screen, concentrating on running and dodging and navigating through the map to try and locate the enemies. But I still hear Jack draw breath in surprise and feel his eyes flick towards me.

"What, for real?"

"Yeah."

He looks back to the screen. We keep on playing. Isn't he going to say anything else?

"Well, that makes sense," he says at last.

"What?"

"I knew something was up. You've been all weird lately. And my mum has too. Like there's some big secret. Anyway, it's good, right? You're really lucky, you know, having a big family. I think it's cool how there's always something going on here, not like at home. Me and Mum and that's it. I mean, all the attention is great, sometimes, but she's always like, what are you doing, Jack? What are you wearing, Jack? Are you all right, Jack? It's too much."

"Yeah," I say, not convinced. Jack has it sorted as far as I can see. Loads more pocket money than me, his mum always around to give him lifts, no younger sisters "borrowing" his things and not putting them back.

"Remember how we'd always boss your sisters around, get them to play schools and battles and stuff, with us in charge?" He laughs. "I mean, plenty of people have really irritating siblings but your sisters are all right."

"It's not that," I say.

"Oh? What then?"

"Mum's not keeping the baby. I'm not getting another sister. Or a brother. She's giving it away."

"What? What are you talking about?" Jack stares at me. He sounds utterly baffled.

"Hey, watch out," I say. "You're gonna lose a life."

"Ah, who cares?" says Jack, deliberately letting himself get surrounded. "What do you mean, she's giving it away? Like putting it up for adoption? But what for? Your mum and dad love kids."

Reluctantly, I give up on the game. I let my character get sniped and the "you lose" screen comes up.

"You know Auntie Jo's friends – Justin and Atif? Well, Mum and Dad's friends too, now. Atif came to the play with us."

Jack nods slowly, still looking confused. "Yeah, what about them?"

"She's giving the baby to them. It's called surrogacy. Like, if you can't have your own kids, someone else can have them for you. That's what Mum's doing."

"You're joking me," says Jack fiercely.

I shake my head. "No joke."

Neither of us say anything for a bit, but I feel like I can hear Jack's mind whirring in the silence. He opens his mouth to speak a couple of times and then shuts it again.

"You know, it makes sense, your mum doing that," he says eventually. "She's always helping people out. But this is something else. Won't that be really sad for you all? Like having a new sibling and then losing them again. I mean, will you even get to see the baby?"

"Yeah, we will, all the time. Mum keeps saying it'll be like having a cousin."

"Oh, well, I guess that's okay then. I'd just find that a bit strange, that's all. I mean, if it was me. When's she having it?"

"Dunno exactly. May? Not for ages."

"Okay, wow. Well, you kept that quiet."

"Course I did, it's embarrassing. I mean, what are people going to say? It's bad enough Mum getting pregnant anyway, when she's so old, but this is worse. Like, what if someone at school finds out? No one else's parents do stuff this embarrassing."

"People at school? You're worried about *them*? Your real friends aren't going to care. That's all that matters."

"It's not that I'm worried about what people think..." I begin.

But then I tail off, because that's not true. I *do* care what people think, especially at school. So far I've kept out of the way of trouble, avoided standing out, and I want to carry on like that. I don't want to become one of those kids that, for some reason, everyone decides is weird so it's okay to pick on or laugh at.

Like Jack, I think, before I can stop myself.

But Jack doesn't notice I've gone quiet. He's obviously thinking about something else. "So, do they pay her?"

he asks finally. "I don't mean it to sound bad, but are they, like, buying the baby off her?"

"No, of course not! Don't be such an idiot." My voice is cracking now. If Justin and Atif are buying a baby, then that means Mum and Dad would be selling one. That sounds awful. "She's just doing it as a favour. That's all, okay?"

But then I start to wonder. I remember Mum telling Justin how expensive it was bringing up kids. I thought she was just joking, but maybe she was serious. Maybe something's wrong and they haven't told us and they really need the money. And what about that thing Bells said, way back when they came for Sunday lunch, that Mum and Dad had been talking with Justin and Atif about expenses? Why were they doing that? What if Jack's right?

"Sorry, mate," says Jack. He sounds mortified. "I didn't mean any offence, honest. I was just asking."

"Well, don't ask," I say. "Anyway, the game's over now. So don't you have to go?"

"Oh," says Jack, looking surprised. "Oh, yeah, okay." He shoves his phone in his back pocket and looks around the room, like he's forgotten something. "See you tomorrow then."

"Yeah," I say, not looking up. "Bye."

He pauses at my door for a moment, waiting. I don't say anything. Then he heads down the stairs and I hear the front door opening. I sit on the floor staring at the blank screen, waiting to hear it slam behind him.

Mum was wrong, I think. I don't feel any better for telling Jack. Not at all. I've just got something new to worry about now – what he said about Mum and Dad getting money for the baby.

But it's ages before I hear the door closing. Instead all I can hear is a murmur of voices from downstairs. Then footsteps coming up and a knock on my bedroom door. It could be Mum, checking if I'm all right. She always used to barge straight in, but since I turned thirteen, she's decided that I need my privacy which is definitely a good thing.

"Yeah?"

"It's me, Ade. Can I come in?"

"Sure," I say. It's not Mum, or Jack coming back up – it's Auntie Jo. It's a surprise, but a good one. "I didn't know you were here."

Auntie Jo slips through the door and sits down on the floor next to me, where Jack was a minute ago.

"I came in just as Jack was leaving," she says. "Your mum's making me a cuppa. I've just been on a run. This was kind of on my way home, so I thought I'd stop in.

I could do with a bit of advice actually." She describes the route to me, and we check the times and distance on her phone and do a few calculations.

"If you keep going like that, you'll definitely do it in under four hours," I tell her.

"Today was only eight miles though, I'm not sure I'll be quite so fast by the time I get to mile twenty-six." She smiles. "But, yeah, I've been working hard and I'm feeling pretty fit. I'm not too worried about getting round the course, especially with all of you lot cheering me on."

"So?"

"Well, it's the sponsorship. I've got to raise £2,000 for my place. At least. That's a heck of a lot of money, isn't it? And it's not like people have got loads of spare cash right now, I feel bad asking."

"But no one will mind," I say. "Not once they know you're running a whole marathon. And, anyway, isn't this kind of like your job? Isn't marketing what you do?" I'm not altogether sure that I've got this right, but this sounds a little bit like marketing to me.

Auntie Jo laughs. "Good point, I suppose it is, but this feels different. At work, I'm selling something for someone else. This is, well, it's about selling me."

"So, I'll help," I say eagerly. It's good to have something to think about which isn't the baby or worrying about

Jack. "I'll be your marketer. We'll start now. Have you set up a web page yet?"

"Yeah, I've done that. Here." She shows me the page on her phone. "It looks a bit sad though." She's right, it does.

"0% of target," I read out loud. "From...zero supporters. Okay, well, we can sort this out. First off, you need to get some decent photos and videos up there. You in your running kit, that sort of thing, and of the baby unit in the hospital. And you definitely need at least one donation before you send this link to anyone. Not just something rubbish, like a fiver, a big one, so people feel like they have to give a bit or they'll look mean. But not so big that they'll get put off."

"You know what?" says Auntie Jo, looking impressed. "You're good. Remind me of this if you're ever looking for a marketing job and I'll write you a reference."

"Let's make a list of everyone you can ask to sponsor you." I open up a new note on my phone. "There's people at work, and any friends on social media, that's obvious. Mum can ask all the people whose kids she looks after and the ones on the PTA."

"Hold on," says Auntie Jo. "I can't ask them, they don't even know me."

"But they know Mum. Mum knows everyone. Anyway,

I bet they all had their babies over at the maternity unit, they'd sponsor you."

"Well, okay," says Auntie Jo, sounding pleased but uncertain. "You're the boss. I've got this list too, that the fundraisers emailed me. It's all the different ways you could raise extra money. Maybe we can get some ideas there." She shows me the list on her phone.

"What's this for?" I ask, confused. "It's all about car washes and cake sales and things. They're not expecting you to organize anything *else*, are they? Isn't it enough to actually run the marathon?"

"Well, let's not worry about that now then. We can crack on with your amazing sponsorship plan and see how that goes."

"Mum can be your first donation, let's go down now and get her to do it," I say, getting up off the floor. "Then you can start sending out the link."

"Oh, I don't know," says Auntie Jo. "I mean, your mum and dad are always so generous, but..."

Was Jack right earlier? Does Auntie Jo not want to ask Mum and Dad to sponsor her because they've got money problems?

"What?" I ask, looking at the floor instead of at her. "Mum and Dad aren't short of money, are they?"

"No, no, of course not."

"Really?"

"Really," she says. "It's just that, what with five kids, you know, it's not like me, single, no responsibilities."

"I guess so."

"You don't sound sure."

"It's just that... I wondered...is that why they're doing this? The surrogacy thing?" Jo looks at me, baffled. I swallow and go on. "Is it because they need the money? I mean, Justin and Atif, they seem pretty loaded and they really want a baby and..."

"No," interrupts Auntie Jo, shaking her head. "No, it's not like that. Even if your parents were worried about money – which they are not, okay? – it's against the law to make money out of surrogacy. So Justin and Atif can pay for some things like, I don't know, transport to the hospital or maternity clothes, anything your mum needs because she's pregnant. But that's all. Got it?"

"Okay," I say.

She puts her hand on my shoulder and gives it a quick squeeze. "But you have given me an idea about who to ask for my first donation. I'll just message Justin now and ask him, what do you think?"

I don't want to say no – it's a good idea – but I also don't like the way things always seem to come back to Justin and Atif. A year ago, we didn't even know them and now, wherever I look, whatever we do, they seem to be there, right in the middle of it. Since they appeared, everything's been changing so fast.

Now that Mum's pregnant, there's no going back to how it was before. Justin and Atif will be part of our lives for ever. Things are going to keep changing, and I'm not sure I'm ready for that.

Chapter Nine

I'm eating a packet of crisps by the bus stop, waiting for Jack to come out of school. Everyone's huddled in their coats against the cold and hurrying quickly through the gates to head home. It's getting dark. Term only started a couple of weeks ago, but already the Christmas holidays seem like ancient history.

School's been rubbish today. The world's most boring assembly. A surprise French test. Mr Milford having a go at me for forgetting my History book. One of those days where nothing goes right. I'm ready for it to be over.

I check my phone. Half past four. Come on, Jack. He's taking ages. Again. Even with PE last thing and getting changed after, he should be out by now. He never used to be late, but last term it started happening more and more. Maybe he doesn't want to walk home with me any more.

Perhaps being friends since we were little isn't enough to stay friends now, and he's trying to tell me something without actually saying it. Since that day in my bedroom when I told him about Mum, things have been weird, awkward. It's always been easy with Jack. Till now. Maybe we're just becoming too different.

I shake my head. No. Jack's still Jack. Still my best mate. If there was something wrong, he'd tell me. With everything changing at home, I don't want to think about things with Jack changing too.

I check Auntie Jo's fundraising page while I'm waiting. She's been doing okay since I took charge of her marketing, but there's still a long way to go before she hits £2,000. I'm trying to think of more ideas, when I spot Jack coming through the gates. It's weird – I'm not sure it's him at first because, instead of his usual walk, which is kind of bouncy, he's trudging slowly towards me.

"Finally!" I say. "What happened? You've been ages."

"Don't give me a hard time today, all right, Aidan? Just…don't, okay?"

I want to ask if he's okay, but something stops me. If he wants to tell me, he will. Won't he?

"Sure," I shrug. "Whatever. Let's go, it's freezing."

I've got a few crisps left. I offer him the bag and he takes a couple.

"Cheese and onion, sorry," I say. I know that's not his favourite. "It's all we've got at home. Mum's eaten all the salt and vinegar ones, since getting pregnant she can't get enough."

He doesn't respond, so I don't say anything either.

Suddenly there's a whistle behind us. I turn and see a group of Year Nine lads with their PE bags slung over their shoulders. They're all from Jack's class.

"Hey, Jack," someone shouts. "Where's your bag, Jack? Lost it again, have you?"

"You need to be more careful!" shouts another voice – I think it's Ethan this time.

It's only now that I notice that Jack doesn't have his PE bag. And that he hasn't got changed – under his jacket he's still wearing his PE kit.

Jack starts walking faster, and I pick up my speed to match his.

"What are they going on about? Why are you still in your kit?" I ask.

Jack just shakes his head and walks even faster.

But however fast we go, Ethan and the others are still there. I can hear them talking and laughing.

Then there's a thump, just behind us.

"Oops, I think you dropped something," calls Ethan. "Aren't you going to run and get it?"

It's a shoe. Jack's shoe.

Jack hesitates, not sure what to do. Neither am I. We can't just leave his shoe there on the pavement, but at the same time, I don't want to hang around and see what else Ethan and the others have got in mind.

"Yeah, Jack," says Sam. "Go and fetch it. We're all waiting to see you run."

"Run…like a girl!" adds Ethan, and there are a few sniggers.

Jack stops and turns round. He walks back slowly and reaches down to pick up his shoe from the pavement, still not saying anything. I feel like I should do something, but I don't know what, so I just stand there.

Just as Jack's getting up, another shoe sails through the air and hits him on the shoulder. Hard. I don't see who throws it, but I can hear them laughing.

"You all right?" I say, grabbing hold of his arm to pull him up. The sooner we get out of here, the better. We just need to take the shoes and run. Although, I realize with a sinking feeling, that if they have Jack's shoes, they've probably got the rest of his clothes too. And what's Jack's mum going to say if he comes home without any uniform?

"Ah, look, his boyfriend's here to help him out this

time. How sweet." A couple of the lads start making kissing noises, and there are a few whistles.

I let go of Jack's arm like it's red hot. They can't think that. They mustn't. "I'm not…" I start. But I can't finish the sentence.

Jack's standing next to me now, a shoe in each hand.

"Come on," I hiss at him. "Let's go. Now."

Jack looks at me. He looks afraid and determined and angry and disappointed. Disappointed in me.

"You can run away if you want, Aidan," he says. "But I'm not running anywhere."

I hover behind him. Everything in me wants to run. But I know I have to stay. I can't leave Jack now.

He takes a step towards Ethan and his mates. "Is that really the best you can do?" he shouts back at them. He's like he is when he's up onstage. He looks bigger, wider, like he's filling the space. "Taking someone else's insults and passing them off as your own? You can't even think of something original to say, is that it?"

There's still a bit of laughter, but it's more awkward now. No one expected Jack to answer back.

"Come on," says Ethan finally. "We've wasted enough time here. Let's go." He turns to me and Jack. "Just be careful who you hang out with, Aidan, people might get ideas. Bye then, have a nice *gay*, I mean, day!" he says and laughs.

Jack stands there, watching as the boys walk off the other way. Left behind them on the pavement is a sports bag. When I'm sure they've gone, I go and pick it up. The zip's undone, and even in the murky evening light, I can see the clothes are streaked with mud.

Jack's not moving, apart from the fact he's shivering. I mean, it's a cold evening, and his PE kit's dead thin, but I know that's not the only reason why he's shaking.

I still don't know what to say, so I don't say anything. I just put Jack's bag on my shoulder, and lightly touch his arm, trying to get him to move. He flinches. I wait.

After a little while, he turns to me. "You didn't go then. I thought you wanted to go."

"I did. I wanted to go. Of course I did." Now that it's all over, I feel anger bubbling up inside me. Anger at Jack. "For god's sake, Jack, what's the point of answering back? It'll only make it worse. What about tomorrow when it's all over school that Jack Ramscombe and Aidan Taylor are gay? What about that?"

"And would that really be the worst thing in the world?" he snaps back.

"Yes," I say. "Yes, it would. I don't understand why you don't just keep quiet and stay out of their way."

"Like you, you mean?" says Jack. "So quiet that no one even knows you exist; you don't let anyone see who you really are. Maybe even *you* don't know, Aidan. But at least I'm not scared of being myself. At least I'm not desperate to be just like everyone else. But I know you, Aidan. You're better than that."

Jack says it like it's a bad thing – trying to fit in – but what's so wrong about that? It's not like I'm hiding anything from the people who matter. Except, I realize in a rush that knocks the breath right out of me, I am. I'm hiding all the time. At home. At school. With Jack.

I feel like I do when I'm running, and I suddenly fall. One second, everything's normal, the next I'm stuck on the ground unable to move. "What do you mean? Who I really am?"

"Oh, never mind, Aidan. Give me my bag. I'm going home."

I've never seen Jack walk this fast before, but even so, I can keep up with him easily. He doesn't look at me though, just stares straight ahead all the way home.

There's one question I want to ask him, but I can't. I just can't.

I want to know if Ethan and everyone's right, whether Jack really is gay or trans or *something*. Is that what he meant when he said he wasn't scared of being himself? I mean, all the signs are there. The way he looks and acts, even the nail varnish. It's like, he *ought* to be gay. And if he is, what does that mean for me? I'm not like that, like him, so does that mean I'm not really gay after all? But if I am, and people find out, then I'll be in the same kind of trouble as Jack. Stares or whispers or worse.

They'd better not find out, that's all.

We reach my house, but Jack just keeps marching on up the hill, without even saying goodbye. I run upstairs and head straight for the shower. I can hear Lily and Bells giggling from behind her bedroom door, but luckily no one's in the bathroom. I lock the door and turn up the water as hot as I can bear.

I reimagine the scene in my head. Instead of just standing there uselessly next to Jack, I step forward and confront Ethan. I tell him to leave my friend alone, and then I punch him. Hard. Like in a film. He falls to the ground and everyone else runs. I run after them and catch them easily. I make them say sorry and promise to leave us alone. But no matter how many times I play it over in my mind, I know it's not what really happened.

I *don't* want to hurt them, not really. I don't even want to make them feel bad. It's like Dad always says, if you use your strength to hurt people, then it's not real strength, just weakness in disguise. Dad's the strongest person I know. When I was little he could pick me up and throw me over his shoulder; I bet he still could now. It goes with being a firefighter. But I know he'd never use that strength to harm anyone else. So why would I want to?

I'm not angry at Jack any more, I'm just angry at myself. I should have stood up for him, not acted like I was ashamed to know him. He's my best friend. I *hope* he's still my best friend. He said I shouldn't try to be like everyone else, because I'm better than that. As if. I've messed it all up. I'm the one who needs to say sorry.

I towel my hair dryish, find some clothes on my floor and throw them on, then run downstairs, two at a time.

I dash through the hallway. Mum sticks her head out of the living room door.

"Hey, Ade, where are you going?" she calls after me. "Don't you ever stop running? Didn't you only just get in from school?"

"Yeah," I say. "Just going over to Jack's, won't be long." I don't want to waste time talking to Mum, I've got to say sorry to Jack, right now, for being such an idiot. If I stop, I'm worried I might wuss out and change my mind.

"Wait, just a sec. Here." And she thrusts a pink cardboard box into my arms. "Give this back to Kelly and say thanks from me while you're there, would you?"

I can't help being a bit curious, even though I'm in a rush. But, even when I peek into the box, I still don't know what it is.

"It's a foot spa," says Mum, seeing my confused face. "My feet have been swelling up, they always do when I'm pregnant." I make a disgusted face at her – I'd be happy if she stopped right there. For once, she gets it and moves on.

"Anyway, Kelly said this might help so she lent it to me. But I don't like it, it feels like someone's tickling your feet. Careful, don't drop it."

"Okay, okay."

It takes longer than the usual one minute and twenty-five seconds to get to Jack's house because of this stupid box. I balance it on one knee while I lean in to ring the doorbell, it slips and I quickly grab it in both hands again as I step back and wait for someone to answer. Eventually Jack's mum comes to the door. She looks flustered.

"Oh, hi, Aidan."

"Hi, can I see Jack?" I ask, trying to peer past her.

"Er..." she says, looking round. "Now's not the best time, I'm afraid. He's a little bit... Well, maybe leave it till tomorrow, okay?"

"But it's urgent," I say.

"Well," she says, shifting from one foot to another and looking uncomfortable. "I'll go and see." Normally Jack's mum would let me in right away. What has Jack told her? That he doesn't want to see me? That I totally let him down? That I'm not his friend any more?

She's back, head peeking out through the barely open door. "Sorry, Aidan, not right now, okay? Say hi to your mum for me." And before I can say anything else, she's shut the door.

I'm still holding the foot spa.

I can't ring the bell again, not after she basically told me to go away, but it feels wrong just to leave it on the doorstep, so I take it home again. Mum's not going to be impressed with me bringing it back though.

I get the box upstairs and shove it under my bed for now, before Mum knocks on my door. I'll take it over some other time.

"You were quick," she says.

"Yeah, well," I say. I can't stop thinking about the look in Jack's eyes when he told me *I* could run away, but that *he* wasn't going to. I wish so badly that I could rewind the last few hours and start again.

"I've got something to show you. It's from the 20-week scan." She pulls out a piece of shiny paper with a blurry black and white smudge on it and presses it into my hand. "Justin and Atif both came along. You won't see them today though, they had to go back down to London straight after. At first the hospital was a bit funny about having them both come in for the scan appointment, but once we explained that they were the dads, it was fine.

I guess they haven't had much experience of surrogacy."

I had totally forgotten that it was Mum's scan today. "Are you all right?" I ask. "And is the..." For some reason it's hard to say the word. "Is the baby all right too?"

"Yes, of course we are. Both right as rain. Nothing to worry about there. Told you, I know what I'm doing!"

I peer at the picture. It doesn't look much like a baby to me.

"Here," says Mum, gently turning the paper round and tracing her finger along the shapes. "Like this, look, there's the head, see?" I nod. "And the legs, all curled up here. I thought it might help to see it, you know, then you'd feel more involved." It's starting to take shape before my eyes. No longer just a blur, but an actual real baby.

"Do you know if it's a boy or a girl?" I ask.

"Ah," says Mum, looking a bit embarrassed. "I do, but I can't tell you, I'm really sorry, love. Justin and Atif don't want to tell anyone, not until after the birth. And, well, it's their baby."

"No one? Not even us?" I say. My voice wobbles a little. I don't know why this makes me feel so upset. Maybe just everything else from today is getting to me.

"I'm sorry," says Mum.

So much for making me feel more involved. This is my brother, or sister, isn't it? Sort of anyway. But it sounds like Justin and Atif want to shut us out of its life before it's even born.

"You'll know soon enough," says Mum, but she can see I'm not happy. "It doesn't really matter that much anyway, does it? It's a healthy baby, that's the most important thing."

"S'pose so," I say. Mum looks like she's getting comfortable at the end of my bed, like she's about to try and start having a heart-to-heart. I am so not in the mood for that.

"Better get on with my homework," I say pointedly to try and distract her.

She sighs, leans down to rub her ankles, and then stands up to go. "All right then. Did you tell Kelly thanks from me?"

"What?"

"For the foot spa, of course. Honestly, Ade, it's like you're on another planet tonight."

"Oh yeah," I lie. "Yeah, I did."

"Oh, and Lily's staying for tea. I'll shout when it's ready."

Since *A Midsummer Night's Dream* and what Atif said about Lily liking me, I've been trying to avoid her, because it feels so awkward. But she seems to be around the house even more than ever.

I don't do my homework once Mum's gone. Of course not. I get the books out of my bag, but I don't open them. I can't keep still. I start pacing round my room, but it's too small and the floor's too covered in stuff to pace very far.

I hate feeling all churned up like this. Knowing Jack's angry at me and there's nothing I can do to make it okay again. Not if his mum won't even let me in to say sorry. I don't remember us ever having fought like this. Sure, we argue about stuff and wind each other up all the time, but nothing that lasts more than a few minutes. Nothing serious.

I pick up my phone, then put it down again. Then a minute later, I pick it up again. I quickly type "*sorry*" and then stop. I'm not sure what to say next. I am sorry that I was too scared to stand up for him after school, but I feel like there's something else I need to say sorry for too, something bigger than just today. I can't find the words for what it is. So I add "*for everything*" and then "*mates?*" which sounds a bit desperate but who cares, and I send it immediately before I can think about it too hard.

I can see straight away that he's read the message, but he doesn't answer. He must still be too angry. Maybe I should just leave it.

At last, just as Mum calls, "Girls, Aidan, come and eat!" up the stairs, my phone goes. I snatch it up.

The message doesn't sound like Jack – no emojis, no pictures, just two letters: *ok*. That's all. But I still feel a surge of relief, even if I'm not totally sure what the message means. Okay what? Okay, he got my message? Okay, he accepts my apology? Okay, we're still mates? Or just okay to everything? But, whatever it means, okay is better than nothing, okay is better than "get lost". If Jack *is* gay, then maybe he's wanted me to ask him about it before. Instead, I've ignored him, shut him down, told him to tone down the way he acts. I pretended it was because I cared about him, but was it, really? Or was it just because I was worried about what people would think of me? It's lonely, not being able to talk to anyone. Maybe Jack feels like that too. Maybe we do need to talk. But where do we start?

Maybe we start right here. I type quickly, so that I don't lose my nerve: *r they right? ru gay?* Send.

I've said it now. I've asked the question. My hands feel sweaty, so I wipe my palms on my trousers.

This time, I don't have to wait ages for a reply. It comes immediately. Just two letters again: *no*.

Disappointment. That's what hits me right away. I think deep down must have always hoped he was, that we'd have this thing in common, that he would understand. Unless he is, but isn't saying because he doesn't feel like he can be honest with me...that would be worse than anything.

I can hear Bells and Lily going downstairs. I'd better follow them or Mum will start hassling me. I throw my phone down on my bed. I'll think about this later. Just as I start to pull my door shut behind me – don't want anyone snooping round my room – my phone buzzes. Another message. I'll just have a quick look.

Two more letters: *ru?*

Chapter Ten

I don't listen to a word anyone says over tea. Mum has to ask me to clear the plates three times before I get up and do anything. It's always a bit of a scramble anyway, with so many of us crammed round the table. Dad's home too, trying to get Lily and Bells to laugh at his jokes – he's on nights this week so won't be at work till later. There's so much going on that I don't think anyone notices how quiet I am. Except maybe Lily, but she's squashed in between Bells and Chloe at the other end of the table, so I can get away with not saying anything to her. I don't feel like eating anyway, my stomach still feels too jumpy.

It's my own fault for starting this, for asking him. I could just ignore his message, pretend I didn't see it. He can't force me to tell him.

But I can't ignore him. Not now. And actually, I don't want to. I don't want to hide anything any more.

Back in my room, Jack's message is still waiting accusingly on my phone. At least I don't have to talk to him face to face. This is easier. I still feel like I'm going to be sick though. I've never said this to anyone. I type three letters: *yes*.

When I press "*send*", my heart's still pounding, but I feel something else too – relief. Maybe Dad's right, it *is* better out than in.

It's slightly longer than one minute and twenty-five seconds before the doorbell rings, but not that much longer. I'm sitting on my bed when Jack sticks his head round the door.

"Okay if I come in?"

"Yeah." I don't say anything else. I'll just wait and see whether he says anything about my message or whether we can just ignore it. I mean, that *must* be why he came round.

He's not wearing his PE kit any more; he's changed into jeans and a jumper. "My mum thinks I'm acting really weird today," he says. "She tried to stop me coming over, I told her that I had to cos you'd got my Science book by mistake. She thought I was too upset after earlier..." I look down at my feet. "She doesn't know exactly what happened, but she's got an idea. I said it was an accident with my school uniform and all that, but she wasn't even cross, so I guess she's worked out something's wrong."

"Has something, you know, like that happened before?" I ask.

"Not like today, but yeah, things have been rubbish, people saying stuff, the lads in my class, they're so..." He stops for a moment, looking for the right word. "So *stupid*. And they just get away with it."

"Why didn't you *say*?" I burst out. "I'm your best friend. You should have told me."

"And then what? You'd have just told me it was all my own fault, that *I* was the one who needed to change."

I don't say anything. He's right.

"I *tried* to just ignore it or laugh it off. I even tried to tone myself down a bit, like you said. But I can't change who I am, or how I look, or walk, or the stuff I like. Or any of the things that they find so funny about me. That's me. And anyway, I don't *want* to change that. Not because of anything some stupid boys say or do. I like who I am." He is standing by my window, looking even taller than usual. I can't see his face, but his voice sounds strong, determined. "Today, standing up to them, it felt so much better than trying to run or hide away."

"I'm sorry," I say.

"I know, it's okay. It's not all about you, Aidan."

"Yeah, but…" I suddenly remember something that Jack said earlier that didn't make sense. "What did you mean about them not even thinking up their own insults?"

"Oh," he says, not sounding strong any more, just worn out. He moves a pile of old running magazines to one side so that he can sit down on the floor under the window. "That. You really want to know?"

I nod. As long as we're talking about Jack, that's fine, because it means that we're not talking about me.

"We had cross-country today, your perfect day, right? I thought at least it would be better than football. But it was still grim. We're running across the field, through the mud and it's freezing. I know you do this all the time, for fun, but that's not normal, is it? I'm right at the back but I don't care. There's Mr Evans shouting away at everyone, except the sporty kids, the ones he likes, they're okay. He's shouting at me the most, telling me to come on, move faster, usual stuff. I think it annoys him that my legs are so long and yet somehow I never seem to get anywhere, like I'm deliberately winding him up. Then, thank god, it's almost over, and everyone else has finished, and they're standing round waiting till I get to the end before we can go in. I guess Mr Evans is cold and tired, like everyone else, even with his thick tracksuit on, and he yells at me 'come on, stop running like a girl'. And Sam and Ethan and everyone crack up, like this is the funniest thing they ever heard."

"No way," I say. "He *can't* say stuff like that, he's a teacher." I can't even begin to imagine what Bells's response to that comment would be. It would blow the roof off. And not just cos she's so loyal to Jack. I can hear her in my mind: listing female Olympic athletes and challenging anyone to say what's wrong with running like a girl in the first place.

"Yeah, well, he *did* say it. He probably did it just to get a laugh, which definitely worked. It certainly wasn't an objective observation about my running style." He pauses, as if he's wondering whether to continue. "And then, I couldn't help it, honest, I stopped running and did this kind of pirouette thing." He stands up and twirls round. "Kind of like this. I thought, he's already had a go at me, what's to lose?"

I bury my face in my hands. "You didn't?" But I know he did.

"Then he *really* kicks off, shouting about how I'm disrespecting him, disrespecting the school, I need to sort out my attitude, he's going to talk to my parents. And it's like showtime, everyone's watching us."

"But that's not fair," I say. Jack can get a bit carried away sometimes, but he'd never deliberately disrespect or be rude to anyone.

"Yeah, well, tell that to Mr Evans. I mean, I don't care about how I look when I'm running, I just hate that he gave everyone an excuse to laugh at me. Like they need it," he says bitterly.

"So what happened to your uniform?" I ask.

"I got everything out of my locker to get changed. I always try to be really careful, cos a couple of times now, someone's grabbed something or hidden it. That's why I'm always late to walk home after PE. I didn't say anything to you before because, well, I was embarrassed, okay? I didn't want to let them get to me. I thought I should be able to deal with it by myself."

He sounds so matter-of-fact now, like he's telling a story about someone else, but I remember how upset he was after school today, how his voice, his walk, everything, made it seem like there was something heavy weighing him down.

"This time, I guess, I wasn't paying attention, I was too wrapped up in thinking about what Mr Evans said, and someone grabbed my whole bag. And before I could get it back, they're throwing my stuff around and kicking it across the muddy floor, laughing like this is a game. I know what they wanted me to do, they wanted me to chase around after it, then they could laugh at me some more. So I didn't, I just left."

He stops, and turns away from me, towards the window. "All that gay stuff is just an easy insult, just because I'm different to them. It doesn't *mean* anything. It doesn't matter if I am or not, it's just another thing they seem to find funny. I'm fed up with it. It's just so *tiring*, you know."

"So, you're not?" I say, after a long pause, forcing the words out.

"No."

"You're sure?"

"Well, pretty sure. I like girls, you know, that's kind of a sign that I'm not." He's smiling, but not in a happy way. "And I don't think I am a girl either, in case you want to ask about that too."

"Okay."

"You thought I was gay?"

"Yes…no…I don't know…" I say, desperately wishing we weren't having this conversation, that I was somewhere, anywhere else. "It's just, I thought, how you act and stuff…"

"I just don't get it," he interrupts. "I don't get why some things are supposed to be okay for girls and not for boys, or the other way round. And there's this invisible line that you shouldn't cross, and if you do the wrong things, then people think you're weird. It's stupid, but everyone seems to think like that. Even the stuff our parents say, you know, without even thinking. Even you, Ade. But why can't people just be allowed to be themselves?"

"I don't know," I say and, just then, I really don't. Everything Jack's said is right, and yet it's too simple. It doesn't feel possible to just be you, not if you don't want people to notice you or look at you funny or try and push you back over to the side of the line where you belong.

"So...what about you?" says Jack slowly, like he's really struggling to find the right words. "I only asked you cos I was so annoyed about you asking me, making out like it mattered what Sam and Ethan and everyone said, I didn't really think you were...but then...in your message...you said...and then it all seemed to make sense."

There's this pressure in my chest, this tightness, like there's something squashing me down and making my head spin and stopping me breathing normally. This is it. The relief that I felt so strongly earlier has gone, now I just feel scared. I don't know what I'm going to say, until I say it.

"Oh," I say. "Oh, that. That was just a joke."

"A joke?" says Jack, sounding confused. "What do you mean, a joke? You mean you're *not* gay? Even though you said you were?"

"No, I'm not." I try to laugh, but it comes out sounding like a strangled cough. "Do I look gay to you?"

It's not exactly a lie, I tell myself, if I'm not a hundred per cent certain. Anyway, just because I've known Jack since we were kids doesn't mean I have to tell him every little thing about my life now. What's the point, when I'm not even sure myself?

Jack shakes his head. "You've known me all your life, haven't you?"

"Er, yeah, almost. So?"

"So I know when you're lying. I'm your best mate, Aidan."

"I'm *not* lying," I insist. "It was just a stupid joke. I didn't know you'd come rushing over when you got the message, did I? I didn't think. I'm sorry."

"Ade," he says, all serious. "What I mean is, you can trust me."

I feel so awkward that I can't sit still any more. I get up and start moving things around on my desk, just to have something to do.

"I know I can trust you, all right? And...you can trust me too. Today, I should have stood up for you, and I didn't and I'm sorry. But if it happens again, it'll be different, I promise. I won't try and run away, okay?"

But the more I keep talking, the less he looks like he believes me. He doesn't say it, but I can see it in his eyes. It's like he's switched off.

"It's late, I'm going home," he says.

"You don't have to," I say quickly. I don't want him to go, not like this. I want to make things okay again, for everything to go back to normal, to how we were. That's the whole point. If I just had a bit more time... "Why don't you stay a bit longer? We could watch TV or something. Text your mum, it's not *that* late."

"Nah, better go." As he walks past my desk, a piece of paper flutters to the floor. He picks it up and stares at it for a moment. "What's this?"

"It's the scan, you know, of the baby. Mum must have left it in here."

"Oh, cool. I've never seen a real one before." He turns it round a few times in his hands like he doesn't know what to make of it. So I lean over and point out the head, the arms, the legs, the tiny dot of the heart, just like Mum did earlier for me.

"Justin and Atif must be well excited," he says, putting the scan gently back down on my desk. "I think it's awesome what your mum's doing for them."

"Yeah," I say. "That's what everyone says. Once their eyes have stopped popping out with surprise."

"Your mum doesn't care what people think though, does she?"

I glance across at Jack's face to see if he's trying to make a point about me, how I shouldn't care what people think either, but I don't think he is. The switched off look he had just a few minutes ago has been replaced by something more thoughtful.

"Guess not," I say. "Sometimes I think she doesn't even care what *we* think, and we're her kids."

"No one's said anything to you at school though, have they? Anything bad about your mum? I mean, if they have...well, she's like a second mum to me."

"No, no one's said anything," I say slowly, realizing with relief that he's right. Maybe I was worried about nothing. "Although that's probably because no one at school knows, no one except you that is. It's not like I'm telling anyone. Anyhow, she doesn't even really look pregnant yet. I guess the only time it would be obvious would be a parents' evening or something."

"Well, if anyone does, you know, say anything, about *anything*, I'm on your side. Okay?"

I feel even worse now. It seems so easy, so obvious when Jack says it, you stick up for your friends, that's what you do. So why do I find it so hard to stick up for him? I can't even tell him the truth about what I'm really feeling.

Jack sighs. "Today's been weird, right? Too much stuff going on. My brain's fried." He presses his hand to his forehead. "I should have realized it was too soon to talk about this, you weren't ready. Anyway, it's okay if you don't want to talk to me. But why don't you talk to Justin or Atif? They're going to be kind of like in your family now, and they seem cool, and they're gay too. I'm sure they'd understand."

I take a step back in surprise, stumbling a little as I bang my heel against the corner of the foot spa box sticking out from under my bed. I don't want to keep it, but if I get it out to give to Jack, he'll ask loads of questions. I don't want to talk to him any more. I want to be by myself. I give the box a kick to push it back underneath the bed, but that hurts my foot even more. I try to make my face blank, totally unreadable, as I say to Jack, "Thanks but I don't want to talk to Justin or Atif. There's nothing for them to understand." I don't want him to stay here any longer. I wish he'd just stop talking and go away.

Once Jack leaves, I can't settle to anything. It's far too late to go for a run. I don't want to do homework or message anyone or go downstairs and watch TV or go to sleep or even just scroll through stuff on my phone.

Finally, I sit down at my desk, fish out an old envelope from a pile of paper and find a pen. At least I can try and get the mess out of my head. Maybe this will help me sort it out.

On the blank side of the envelope, I write "Am I gay?"

I underline it twice and draw a line down the middle. On one side, I write "for" and the other side "against".

Then I stare at the empty space for a couple of minutes and chew the end of my pen.

Five minutes later, I've written:

For

1. I've never kissed a girl (Poppy Rutherford was my girlfriend in Year Six for about three weeks but all we did was hold hands which was boring and her hands were always a bit sticky).
2. The way my stomach kind of flips over when I see W (I write "W" instead of "Will" in case someone sees, which is stupid, because if anyone reads this list I'll die of shame anyway, but I still do it).
3. My obsession with one of the Blue Peter presenters when I was little (embarrassing but true, whenever the twins are watching and I hear the theme tune I still always think about his smile).

Against

1. I'm not into rainbows, or pink, or glitter (although I don't think that's a rule or anything).

2. I've never kissed a boy (but, I know, as I finish reading through this stupid list, that only one thing matters – that I want to).

I quickly fold the envelope over, so the writing's hidden, even from me. Then I shove it as far away as I can, under the foot spa box beneath my bed. There, gone. I'm not going to think about that any more.

MARCH

Chapter Eleven

"Big one next weekend, twenty miles, then I just have to ease off for the next few weeks till the day itself," says Auntie Jo, her leg propped up against the wall outside our house. We've just finished a run and we're doing stretches to cool down.

I know going running with your aunt is a bit of a sad thing to do, but I love being out on a run with Auntie Jo. Just the two of us, spurring each other on, winding each other up and talking about anything and everything. Anyway, I've always thought that if I see anyone from school, I can drop behind and let her put some distance between us. But today I feel bad about even thinking like that. What does it matter what anyone else thinks? And why would they care anyway? Although I do still check over my shoulder sometimes, just in case I spot someone I know.

She groans and switches legs. "I can't say I'm going to miss the training when this is all over." But she's grinning, I know she loves running as much as I do, never mind if it's cold and rainy. "Haven't you got a big race coming up soon too?"

"Not for a few weeks, but, yeah, if I finish anywhere in the top three, I'll have enough points for a real chance at the Under-14s cup."

I remember when I first started at the club, four years ago, one of the youngest, dreaming that I could be a cup winner one day. But I've never been good enough, not till now. I try not to think about it too much in case that jinxes it and I flake out in the next race, especially after messing up last year's Under-13s.

"I'll never understand how they work out the winners," says Auntie Jo, shaking her head.

"It's easy," I explain for the hundredth time. "If you're in the club, you get points in each race depending on what position you finish, okay? The points you get in your top five races count towards the cup. So what matters is not just one race, it's how good you are across the whole season. You need to do well every time. Every race matters. Simple. The next one's only a few miles away from home, so Mum and Dad say they're going to come and watch."

"Is it okay if I come too? They can give me a lift. That's the week before the marathon, so I only need to do a short run that weekend. It'll be a treat to watch someone else doing the hard work."

"Sure," I say. "Want to come and see what real running's like, do you?"

"Cheeky," she says. "Like to see you run a marathon."

"Maybe one day I will," I say. "Then we'll see who's fastest."

She looks at me for a moment. "That's just the sort of thing Justin would say, same competitive streak. You know how we became friends, don't you?"

I shake my head. I'm not sure I like Auntie Jo comparing me to him.

"It was this work Christmas quiz, all the different offices together. He and I were on the same team. It didn't take long for us to realize that we were the most competitive people there. Everyone else just wanted to slope off to the bar, but the two of us, we really wanted to win!"

"And did you?" I ask.

"Of course," says Auntie Jo. "He's great on music trivia and I bring an encyclopaedic knowledge of capital cities – we're the dream team. No one really cared about who won though, apart from the two of us."

Sometimes I forget that Justin was Auntie Jo's friend first. I wonder how she feels about the whole surrogacy thing, if she ever expected something like this to happen. I'm about to ask her, when Mum sticks her head out of the front door and says, "Are you two ever coming in? Or will you carry on gossiping on the doorstep all evening? Kettle's on." Then she disappears inside again.

I knew Justin and Atif would be here when we got in, sitting on the sofa like they're right at home. I knew they would be here, because they're here more and more now it's getting closer to Mum's due date, just two months to go.

They stay over at Auntie Jo's when they come up, but they're mostly round our house. And it's kind of okay, them being here. We're used to each other. It's like we've found an arrangement that works. We're polite, but we don't talk about anything that matters. It's just stuff like the weather or what's on TV or how things are going at school.

It's not hard to keep my distance when the house is always full of other people talking and laughing and shouting, and the twins treating Justin and Atif like their own personal climbing frame. And, anyway, Justin and Atif are too wrapped up in thinking about the baby to pay much attention to me. I don't worry so much any more that they'll suspect I'm gay. I've hidden it too well. From them, and from everyone else. Neither Jack nor I have said anything about me coming out to him, not since I told him it was all a joke. It's almost like that whole conversation never happened. Except sometimes I look back at the messages and wonder if I did the right thing.

Auntie Jo showers first, then me, then we grab slices of cake from the kitchen and squeeze in next to everyone else in front of the telly. I'm so ravenous that I feel like I could eat the whole cake. Training with the club this morning, and the run just now as well. It feels good to be warm and dry and relaxed. There's this reality TV show we all watch together every week. At the start of the series, we each picked a different contestant to support. Mine's on the edge of being knocked out, and I want to see if they manage to scrape through or not this week.

Jack's here too, as usual. Since he and Bells both got main parts in *The Lion, the Witch and the Wardrobe*, they've been hanging out a lot at rehearsals. They are both big fans of this show too, so Jack always comes round to watch with us. He and Bells chat all the way through about the costumes, the dances and who they think is going to win.

Bells probably spends more time with Jack at the moment than I do. He and I have got out of the habit of walking home together. I've been training, doing more races, and he's been busy with the play. And even when we are together, it's not the same. It's like there's an invisible wall between us. As far as I can tell, the bullying's stopped. I mean, I've not seen anything, and Jack's not said anything. But maybe I'm wrong and it hasn't. Maybe he just doesn't want to talk about it with me. As soon as we settle down to watch, Auntie Jo's phone beeps.

"Ooh," she says, checking her messages. "Another donation's just come in. Justin, it's from Qasim, do you know him? He's the new guy in Sales in the Sheffield office. Oh, isn't that kind, he hardly knows me."

"Hmm, is he the cute one, with the big brown eyes?" says Justin. I stare at the TV, pretending to be absorbed in what's going on to stop myself blushing.

"Yeah," laughs Auntie Jo. "That's the one."

"How are the donations going?" asks Mum, helping herself to a handful of salt-and-vinegar crisps. She's not eating cake like the rest of us, but she scoffs crisps all the time now. She says it's not because she's greedy; it's because it's a pregnancy craving.

"I don't know. I've asked everyone I can think of and I'm still about five hundred quid short. There's not a lot of time. It'll take more than this tenner from cute Qasim to reach the target. Aidan's really helped though. I wouldn't have got anywhere without him."

"There must be *something* else we can do," I say, taking another huge bite of cake. "Another shout out on social media? A final countdown to the race?"

"Aidan," says Mum. "Don't talk with your mouth full, there's cake crumbs everywhere now."

"There's not!" I protest, brushing the crumbs off my lap onto the floor. "Anyway, your crisp crumbs are going all over the place too." I lick my finger and run it over my plate to get the last sugar hit from the icing. That's what gives me the idea. "Hey, why don't you do a cake sale, like in that list of ideas the hospital sent you. Remember? All the info to organize it will be in there. Bells would help too. Wouldn't you, Bells? We could all make stuff."

Mum snorts. "I know you're an expert in *eating* cake, Ade, but since when have you ever made one?"

I shrug. "Can't be that hard. Anyway, we've done it in Food Tech before."

"Lily and I could make brownies. You could make us some signs for it, couldn't you, Jack? You're really good at art," says Bells.

"Course I can, fliers too if you like," says Jack.

"That'd be ace. See, Bells and Jack are up for it. And you make the best cakes, Mum," I say, looking up at her.

"It's true."

"Now you're just trying to sweet-talk me," she says, but I can tell she's pleased.

"We could definitely bake something if you need it," chips in Atif. "I can do my famous lemon-frosted cupcakes."

"They *are* delicious," agrees Justin. "I can't believe we haven't made them for you before. We can put that right when you come and..." Mum shoots him a look.

"We haven't talked about that properly yet," she says firmly. Before I can work out what that's about, her expression changes. "Hey," she says suddenly, leaning forward in her seat and rubbing her bump. "Baby's busy tonight, like it's dancing away to all this music. Lads, come and see if you can feel a kick."

Justin and Atif look at each other uncertainly.

"You're sure?" says Justin.

"Course," says Mum. "It's your baby, isn't it? Come on."

I don't know how we've gone from talking about cupcakes one minute to the next minute, Justin and Atif leaning over Mum, pressing their hands on her bump. But that's what's just happened.

"Oh," says Justin suddenly. "Was that...? It was so quick." His face looks like it's been lit up from inside. "Atif, did you feel it?" Atif nods. He looks a little bit stunned. I don't know what they seem so surprised about.

I mean, they knew there was a baby in there, right?

"You can sometimes even see the outline of the foot," says Mum. "When this little one gives me a really good kick."

"Mum, ssh, that's the grossest thing I ever heard!" I protest.

Luckily Auntie Jo comes to my rescue.

"Just going back to this cake sale idea, it all sounds great," she says. "And I do really appreciate it, but where am I going to sell all these amazing cakes you're going to make?"

"That's easy," I say. "We could have a stall at the next race in a few weeks. Everyone's always starving after a race. I bet you'd sell loads. And you could get sponsors as well."

"Do you think the organizers would be up for that?" she asks.

"I can ask," I say. "I'll email now if you like."

"What do you reckon, Laura, Pete? I'd need your help," Auntie Jo asks Mum.

She's interrupted by a big cheer from the TV audience, but only Chloe's still watching properly, so the rest of us have got no idea why they're cheering. I decide that the cheering is an endorsement of my great idea.

"Sounds like a lot of work," says Mum doubtfully. She looks at all our faces, then smiles. "But why not? We've got the team. You'll make your banana bread, won't you,

Pete?" Dad nods his agreement. "One condition though, if I'm supposed to be behind this stall selling cakes to hungry runners all day, I want one of them fold-up chairs to sit on."

"Done!" says Jo. "I just better not eat too much of that cake myself, however tempting. It's all healthy food for me in the week before the marathon."

"Don't worry, Jo," says Justin. "We'll do our bit for the team by eating your share of cake."

"Thanks a lot!"

"And we'll have a big slice waiting for you at the finish line."

"That's more like it."

"You're going to be there? You're going to watch the marathon too?" I ask.

Typical, I think, Justin and Atif muscling in again, like they are more important to Auntie Jo than we are. Mum and Dad haven't said what our plans are, but they know how much I want to go and they haven't said anything about *not* going, so…

"We'll definitely be there," says Atif. "The start's only a few miles from our flat."

"We always go and watch," adds Justin, "Although this year will be extra-special as we'll be there for Jo of course." He and Atif exchange looks. "In fact, we wanted to ask you something..."

"Listen, Aidan," cuts in Mum abruptly. "I know you had your heart set on us all going to the marathon and cheering Jo on. And if things were different, I'd be right there. Family always comes first, you know that. But look at me..." She pats her bump. "In a month's time I'll be out of breath waddling down the street, let alone standing all day by the side of the road or nipping along to different points on the route..."

"And it would be a right long day for Daisy and Evie, with school the next day," chips in Dad. "And there'll be big crowds. It'll be a bit much for your mum by herself. I need to be on shift that weekend, so I can be off for the birth in May and..."

I've heard enough excuses. "What?" I burst out. "That's so not fair."

I glare at Justin and Atif. It's all their fault. If Mum wasn't pregnant, this wouldn't even be an issue.

"I could still go though, couldn't I?" I insist. "I'd pay for the train ticket. I'd be fine by myself." I try to sound confident, but I can't honestly imagine Mum and Dad agreeing to this plan. I'm still only thirteen.

"I've got a better idea," says Justin, sounding smug, like he knows it all.

"No thanks," I say, still glaring at him. "You're not part

of this family. We don't need your ideas. It's not any of your business."

"Hey, he's just trying to help," says Jack.

"Sssh," says Chloe fiercely, shuffling closer to the TV and putting her arms around Toto's neck. "Stop shouting, I'm trying to watch the programme."

Justin holds up his hands like he's trying to calm everything down. "No, fair enough, that's okay. All I was going to say is that – and only if you want to of course – well, is that you and Bells would be really welcome to come and stay with us that weekend." He finishes in a rush, like he's worried we're going to turn him down. "We've been waiting for the opportunity to invite you down, and your mum's right, it might be a bit much for the whole family. Jo's staying with her old uni friends, so we've got the space to fit you in."

"Oh," I say.

"Seriously?" says Bells. "That's awesome. Could we go on the London Eye too?"

"Bells…" says Mum sternly. "It's very kind of Justin and Atif to offer to have you to stay, don't make them want to change their minds."

"Oh, I mean, thanks…" Bells pauses. "What about Madame Tussauds? That would be so cool. Lily's got this picture of her with Ariana Grande from when she went.

She looks so real."

"Er...maybe, why not?" says Justin, looking more relaxed now. He turns to me. "What do you think, Aidan?"

"Stay with you? For the marathon?"

"Yeah. It would be a good chance to get to know each other better too. You could see how we're getting on with decorating the nursery."

"Just Aidan and Bells?" asks Chloe, turning away from the TV.

"I'm afraid we only have room for two," says Atif. "Sorry, Chloe, we'd really like to do something special with you and the twins another time." He turns to Jack. "And, of course, we'd squeeze you in too if we could, Jack. We know you're like part of the family."

"No worries," says Jack, grinning.

"Why does everyone *always* forget about me?" mutters Chloe. "It's always all about Aidan and Bells. You think I'm just a baby, like the twins, but I'm not."

"No one thinks you're a baby," says Mum soothingly.

"Yes, you do, you all do," says Chloe, sounding choked up. We're all staring at her in surprise now. It's not like Chloe to get upset about something like this. "I'm going upstairs."

"But you'll miss the programme," says Mum. "It's nearly the results bit."

"I don't care," shouts Chloe and stomps out. Toto

uncurls from the floor, shakes herself, and follows Chloe upstairs.

"Family life," sighs Mum, rolling her eyes at Justin and Atif. "I'll go and see if she's okay." She pushes herself out of her chair, wincing a little bit.

"Maybe we should go now," says Atif. "What do you think, Jo? We don't want to cause any trouble."

"No," says Mum. "Don't be daft. You stay right there."

No one says anything. We all just stare at the screen. I'm thinking about what it would be like staying with them in London for the marathon. It's ideal, but at the same time, it feels like Justin and Atif are taking over. Again. I don't want to have to feel grateful to them for anything. And it would be so awkward. We can't just talk about the weather and what's on TV for a whole weekend. Although with Bells there I wouldn't have to worry too much about filling the silence. Whatever, I guess it's better than being stuck at home only able to watch the race on TV.

I'm also a bit intrigued about what their flat's like – I would kind of like to see it – and what their life's like when they're not with us. I think it's quite different from our life or Mum and Dad's friends or people at school, although I don't really know how. I could always just ask them about it, I suppose, but I don't want to.

"Well, I think it's a great idea," says Auntie Jo. I'd

almost forgotten she was here. "Even if the whole family can't come, I'd love to have you both there. Chloe will calm down. Please, Aidan, think about it."

I take a deep breath. I'm not sure what to do. I do want to go, so badly, and the only way to do that is to stay with Justin and Atif, whether I like it or not. Plus, Auntie Jo wants us to come, she'll need our support. It would be stupid to refuse to go, but I still don't want to sound too keen.

"Oh, all right then," I mutter.

Bells claps her hands together. "Awesome!"

Justin smiles nervously at me.

I'm only doing it because Auntie Jo asked, I tell myself. This race is about her, not me. And certainly *not* about Justin and Atif.

APRIL

Chapter Twelve

Atif has come good on his promise.

"Here, Daisy, Evie, one for each of you. Can you hold them nice and steady all the way there?" he says, leaning through the back door of the car and balancing a tin of iced lemon cupcakes on each twin's lap. They both have their serious faces on, concentrating hard on keeping the cakes absolutely still. I am squashed in the middle between the two booster seats. I am tempted to open one of the tins and take a cupcake, but the twins are guarding them so fiercely that I wouldn't get away with it.

The boot's full of cakes and biscuits. We spent all day yesterday making them. Auntie Jo did a run and came back before we'd even finished the first two batches. It was fun, despite Bells bossing us all around, but I'd still rather have been out running. We've also packed Jack's signs, some collecting tins and, as promised, a fold-up chair for Mum. There's not space for all of us in our car today with all the extra stuff packed in – there's barely room for me to cram my kit under my feet – so Bells and Lily are going with Justin and Atif. Jack's mum is taking Jack, Chloe and Auntie Jo.

"Go on, it'll be fun," I hear Bells saying to Justin in her most charming voice. "What's the point of having a convertible if you don't take the roof off?" It's starting to drizzle, so I don't think he's going to say yes. I just hope their flash car doesn't get *too* covered in mud.

I feel awkward turning up with so many people in tow. It's normally just me at a race or, at most, Mum or Dad dropping me off and then waving goodbye without getting out of the car. They're pretty low key events anyway.

I lean forward and whisper to Dad as he settles behind the wheel. "You're not to be embarrassing, okay?"

Dad pretends to be offended. "Here I am to support my only son, to cheer him on, show him how proud I am of him and all he's worried about is me embarrassing him."

"Yeah, exactly, so don't. It's a race, not primary school sports day."

"Those were good days," says Dad. "Remember them parents' races? I was a bit faster on my feet back then..."

"Yes, I do remember them," I say quickly. "That's what I'm talking about. Just keep a low profile today, okay? You can be as embarrassing as you like at Chloe, Evie and Daisy's sports days, just not today."

"All right. Your mum and Jo will keep me out of trouble anyway. We'll be right busy, what with all those cakes we've got to sell, and keeping an eye on your little sisters." His eyes meet mine in the rear-view mirror. "Seriously though, I *am* proud of you, you know that, don't you? Not just with your running. This cake sale business, all your idea."

I hope he's not going to start a heart-to-heart, especially when it's almost time to go.

"Thanks, Dad." I sit back in my seat, then spring forward again as I remember one more thing I need to say. "And if people ask you who Justin and Atif are, just say they're friends of you and Mum, okay? You don't have to tell them the whole story."

Dad sighs. "Okay, Ade, if that's what you want…"

"Yes, it is. And you're definitely *not* to mention Team Rainbow."

Mum heaves herself into the passenger seat and tucks the seat belt under her bump. "Sorry, I'm here at last, let's get going." She leans back and shuts her eyes. "I feel like a beached whale. I think I might have overdone it a little yesterday, all that baking and rushing around getting everything ready for the cake sale today," she says.

"Are you all right, love?" asks Dad. It's not like Mum to *ever* admit to doing too much. I study her face in the mirror. She does look a bit pale. "I can cope today if you need to go and lie down."

"No, no, don't fuss. I'll just take it easy now. I'll be fine."

It's only a short drive, but by the time we get there, Mum does look much better. We've come early to set up the stall, so apart from us, it's just the marshals and a handful of the keenest runners. The drizzle's stopped and the sun is breaking through the clouds. The conditions look pretty good.

Daisy and Evie find a huge puddle and compete to see who can make the biggest splash, while Dad and I ferry cakes out of the car. I don't worry too much about making the stall look good, because I know when Jack and Bells get here, they'll completely reorganize it anyway.

"Well, well, this is something, isn't it? Bit better than our usual, and such a good cause," says Charlie's dad, clapping his hands together. "Everyone at the club likes to show some community support when we can." He beams, takes a note out of his wallet and shoves it into the top of one of the collecting tins.

"It's all a team effort!" says Dad cheerfully. "Not a lot to do with me. I'm just the driver, you know, it's my sister-in-law who's the marathon runner, over there, just getting out of the car now. I think that's where our Aidan gets it from."

I have a sudden flashback to that meal at "Wok Around the Clock", the last time I saw Dad and Charlie's dad in conversation – that moment still fills me with horror whenever I remember it. I hope Dad isn't going to choose now to give his promised explanation of how Mum got pregnant.

But before he has a chance, Charlie's dad strides off energetically to greet Auntie Jo. It looks like she's trying to thank him and he's trying to wave her thanks away.

Lily and Bells pile out of Justin and Atif's car and walk over arm-in-arm, before fussing over the stall. Justin and Atif are standing very close together, looking a bit out of place in their clean wellies, but they're not holding hands or anything. Good. Nothing to make people stare.

Now everyone's arriving and we even have a few customers.

"Laura, why don't you sit down? Take the weight off your feet," says Justin, looking concerned as Mum flits around, laughing and chatting to everyone.

"Thanks, but I'm fine, honestly." Justin doesn't look

happy, but he doesn't say anything. None of his business. Except it kind of is, I suppose; it's his baby that Mum's carrying. I do wish she *would* sit down though, not because of Justin but because she still looks really pale.

However, Mum is our biggest attraction. Other people's mums keep coming over to ask her when she's due, tell her how well she looks and to share their own stories of the maternity unit. It's a bit embarrassing, but it's working, along with the posters that Jack designed. We've already sold loads of cakes, and the collecting tins are starting to get heavy.

"Do you mind?" I ask Auntie Jo. "No one's asking you about the marathon, just talking to Mum about babies."

"Story of my life," she replies. "Not that *you'd* know what it's like being a younger sibling." But she doesn't look like she minds at all. "I'm like you, Aidan, I'm usually happier *not* being the centre of attention. What time does your race start anyway?"

"Eleven o'clock, isn't it?" says a voice behind me. I hadn't even noticed Lily was there, but suddenly she's right next to me. "After the Under-13s set off."

"Yeah, that's right."

"Good luck and everything," she says, blushing a little.

"Er, thanks," I say. And then, because it's the first thing that pops into my mind, I ask "How's Will?"

Lily looks surprised that I'm asking. "Oh, he's okay. I guess. Hardly ever see him. He's always round his girlfriend's. Mum says he might as well move in there."

"His girlfriend?" I ask. My mouth has gone dry and I have to cough to clear my throat. I bet now I've gone red too.

"Yeah, you know. Jen Thomas."

Of course, the girl I'd seen him with at *Midsummer Night's Dream*.

"You all right?" says Lily, peering at me.

"Yeah, er, fine. I'd better, you know, just..." And I nod towards Charlie and a group of other runners standing near the start of the course.

"Okay, good luck," she says again.

I wander off, making my way slowly towards the others. Of *course*, Will has a girlfriend. This is hardly shock news. If you're that fit... I shake my head to try to settle my thoughts down. Why should I care if he does anyway? It's not like him and me...but I can't even think it, it's so ridiculous.

I can't let this put me off. It's already extra pressure knowing that Mum and Dad are going to be watching at the start. I've got to stay focused. Remember last year. No, don't remember it. Only think about now. My stomach feels tight with nerves.

Once the race actually starts, it's fine. More than fine. I feel my muscles stretch and my chest burn as I push myself towards the front of the field. Even with other runners all around me, even knowing my whole family and more are here today, chatting and eating cake, I feel like it's just me and the hills. I feel free out here. I want to win. I want to get the points so that, when they add all the scores up, I've got a good chance of winning the cup at the end of the season. But most of all, I want this – this feeling – to go on for ever.

The last few metres pass in a blur. I pass a couple of runners I recognize, and a few more I don't. They must be from other clubs. I see Jon, who won the Under-13s last year. We've each picked different routes to get here, but now we're drawing level. We can both see the finishing marker up ahead. There's a few people hanging around there. I spot Auntie Jo with Jack, who's wiping the rain off his glasses. Then I see Chloe and Bells and Lily too. They must all have left Mum and Dad in charge of the stall. And seeing them gives me the last burst of speed I need, moving fast but carefully on the slope, so as not to trip over at the last minute. I'm there. I've finished. I bend over, breathing heavily. My legs ache, but I don't care. I'm buzzing.

Auntie Jo's grinning at me.

"Told you," I gasp, still trying to catch my breath.

"Told you I'd show you what real running's like."

"You did that," she says, still smiling. "I'd like a finish like that next Sunday. Well done, Aidan. I *would* give you a hug but..." I see her taking in my sweaty, muddy kit.

"It's okay," I say. I'm quite happy to remain unhugged now. I'm too excited to stand still for long enough anyway.

"You actually won," says Jack excitedly. "Against all those people. You were well ahead. This means you get the cup, right?"

"Not quite," I say. "But, yeah, I've got a really, really good chance. Just one more race to go."

"That's brilliant!" says Jack. His voice is different. He sounds like the old Jack, not guarded or distant like he's been with me for the last few months, but genuinely happy for me. "Although I still can't understand why *anyone* would do something like that for fun," he continues. "Just look at you."

Auntie Jo's phone starts ringing. "That's odd," she says, staring at the screen. "Why's your dad ringing me? He's only just over the other side of the car park. Maybe he wants the up-to-the-minute race report. He's going to be so proud of you."

She answers, "Hey, Pete, you all right? Aidan came in like lightning... Yeah, he's finished the race now and... Yeah, of course Bells is with me too. What is it?" Then she goes quiet for a long time. I can hear the buzz of Dad's voice on the other end of the line, but not what he's saying. I can tell it's something serious though by the way Auntie Jo is biting her lip. We all can.

"No problem," she says finally. "Of course, you go. We'll be fine. No, really, don't worry."

"What?" asks Bells as soon as Auntie Jo finishes the call. "What is it?"

"It's your mum," she says, and my stomach drops. She sees my expression. "No, it's nothing to worry about. Your dad just needs to take her into the hospital now."

"The hospital? Why? What's wrong?" I exclaim.

"She thinks her waters have broken," says Auntie Jo.

"What? What is that?" I have no idea what she's talking about. The only word she's said that makes any sense is "hospital".

"It normally happens when the baby's nearly ready to come, but this is a little bit early, so your dad just needs to take her in so they can look her over." Auntie Jo's voice is low and soothing, the way adults make their voices go when they are worried about something but don't want you to think they are.

I didn't think I had any running left in me, but the adrenaline comes back in a rush. I start sprinting towards the stall.

"But the baby *isn't* ready to come yet!" I hear Bells say. "It's not going to be ready for another five weeks."

"Hold on," shouts Jack after me. "Wait up, we're not all top-level athletes." But I ignore him and keep on running.

When I get to the stall, Jack's mum and Atif are there, dishing out cakes to mud-splattered runners, but there's no sign of Mum and Dad. Have they already gone?

Then I spot them in the car park. I keep on running till I reach our car. Mum's getting in, Dad's calmly removing Daisy's and Evie's car-seats and handing them to Justin, who looks like he can't keep still. But Mum looks fine. No different from earlier. So why are they going to the hospital in such a rush?

Because Dad's a firefighter, he's really good at keeping cool in an emergency; I can't tell from his expression how serious or not this is.

"Hey, Aidan," says Mum, turning as I run up behind her. "How was the race? You look like you've been rolling in the mud, not running through it."

"Yeah, fine, I won, whatever," I rattle out. That seems like the least important thing in the world right now. "Are you okay?"

"You won? Aidan, that's brilliant."

"Come on, Laura," says Dad. "Let's go. I've sorted it all out with Justin."

"Are you *sure* we shouldn't come, one of us at least?" Justin asks Dad, leaning forward, holding a car-seat in each hand.

Dad looks exasperated. Mum lays a hand on his arm.

"Look, Justin, we'll call you as soon as we know more, and you'll be right there the moment anything happens. I just need to be checked out, that's all. My waters breaking before labour's started, well, that's a bit unusual. But then I'm sure I'll be right back home. The best thing you can do for us is make sure the kids get back okay."

Justin looks doubtful, like he's about to say something else but has changed his mind at the last minute.

"I know this is your baby and I know you're worried," says Mum softly. "I'm so glad you're nearby, not down in London, but save your energy, there's no need for all of us to spend hours hanging round the hospital, there will be plenty of time for that."

"But Mum?" I interrupt.

"I'm fine," she tells me, as she climbs into the car. "I've taken a few slices of cake to keep us going if we have to wait for ages. Can you tell Jo that I'll put in the money tomorrow? I'll see you later."

I should feel reassured. But I still don't feel like I understand what's going on. Mum looked well. Dad seemed calm. Justin, however, looks a wreck.

I hear panting behind me. I turn.

"Jack?"

He just nods. He's red in the face.

"You *ran* after me?"

He nods again.

"Wow," I say. "You never run anywhere."

"Wanted to see...if you were...all right. Is everything okay with your mum?" he asks breathlessly.

"I think so," I say. "She says she's just going to the hospital to get checked over, whatever that means."

"Okay, good, so we don't have to deliver the baby here in a field? Cos I've watched a lot of hospital dramas, but..."

Justin looks alarmed. I don't think he's in the mood for jokes.

"No, you muppet," I say to Jack, feeling much better now I've seen Mum looking all right, and Jack's here. "Course not."

"Cake, then?" he asks. "Before my mum sells it all."

I am suddenly ravenous. "One hundred per cent," I say.

Chapter Thirteen

There are fifteen people in our house right now. And a dog. I just counted. Fifteen people – but no Mum and Dad. They're still at the hospital. It feels as if they've been gone for hours. If Mum was just being "checked over", as people keep saying, then surely she'd be home by now.

I don't remember anything about when Bells or Chloe were born, I was too young. Even when Mum went into hospital to have the twins, I was only six or seven. The main thing I remember is that when Auntie Jo came to look after us, she brought the biggest packet of jelly babies ever and let us watch loads of TV. The next day, we went into the hospital to see Mum, who looked worn out but very pleased with herself, and we took lots of photos. I remember feeling disappointed that even though she'd had two babies this time, neither of them was a brother for me.

Back then, I was just a kid, I had to rely on adults to tell me what was going on. Now, I can google it on my phone. I don't know what "waters breaking early" means, so I look it up, then I wish I hadn't. It's not just that everything about giving birth makes me feel a bit squeamish, it's that it seems like this could put Mum and the baby in danger.

The "waters" aren't even water, which is confusing enough, it's the stuff the baby floats around in while it's growing. When it's ready to be born, this liquid's not needed any more, so it kind of seeps out. Yuk. That's called the waters breaking. Except Mum's baby *isn't* ready to be born. It still needs all this liquid to keep it safe and healthy. So I think this means either the baby's got to come now or the doctors need to find a way to keep it safe inside Mum for a bit longer.

The info I find is all written in the same let's-all-stay-calm-nothing-to-worry-about tone that Auntie Jo's been using since the phone call with Dad. It's driving me mad. This isn't normally the way she talks, not to me.

It felt wrong to hang around too long at the race, but wrong to go home straight away as well. After all, there were still runners finishing and people keen to buy cake.

And I knew Mum would tell us off if we didn't do our best to sell it all. It would be just like her to carry on organizing everything remotely, even from a hospital bed.

Between Jack's mum, Charlie's dad and Justin, there was enough space in the cars to get us all home, but now everyone's still here. In fact, even more people have arrived since we got back. Lily's mum came to collect her, but instead ended up in the kitchen with Jack's mum, making cups of tea for everyone else. No one seems to want to leave until there's news from Mum and Dad. If you didn't know better, you'd think it was a party. Mum and Dad would love having this many people round the house. If they were here.

"I make that £230.62," says Charlie's dad, sorting the notes and coins into neat little piles on the kitchen table. "Agree?"

"Yeah, I think so." I'm sitting opposite him, checking the piles as he counts. It's good to be able to focus on something. "And some random foreign coins."

"That's a pretty good result from one morning's work. Nearly as impressive as your result in the race."

"It's amazing," says Jo, putting her hand on my shoulder. I'm still in my sweaty, muddy kit, but she doesn't seem bothered any more. I desperately want to be by myself, but I don't want to go for a shower in case I miss a call from Mum or something. "I'm only a couple of hundred short of the total now."

"Why don't I top it up for you?" says Justin.

"What?"

"I'll donate the balance, whatever you need to meet your target."

"Justin, that's kind, really, but you don't have to."

"Think of all the times we've stayed at your flat these last few months, it's the least I can do. I just want to, you know..." He stops and looks down at the table, clenching and unclenching his fists, before continuing fiercely, "I just want to be able to *do* something." He suddenly turns away without waiting for Auntie Jo to answer and rushes out of the kitchen.

I sit with Auntie Jo and Charlie's dad for a bit, but my head's beginning to ache. I know they think they are helping, but why can't everyone just go home and leave us alone?

Perhaps I'll feel better if I do have a shower; it will only take a few minutes. I pick my way through the people. I feel like I can breathe better the further I get from the busyness of the kitchen and living room. I start to climb the stairs but freeze when I hear voices at the top. Justin and Atif have obviously had the same idea about getting away from the bustle downstairs.

"I can't help it," says Justin, sounding anxious. "I mean, you didn't hear them, it was like they didn't want us to be there. Of course I'm worried."

"Just breathe," says Atif soothingly.

"Why isn't Pete answering his phone? It just goes straight to voicemail every time I try. What if Laura's in labour already and we miss the birth? It's our baby – we should be there. That's what we agreed right at the start. If there's even a tiny risk of something going wrong, we need to be there, working out what to do together. Come on, why can't he just pick up the phone? They don't want to talk to us, I know it."

"Or they've got no reception, or have run out of battery, or maybe they are seeing the doctor right now. It could be anything. They'll call us. Okay? They trust us, in their house, with their kids, they couldn't trust us more. So we've got to trust them with our baby."

I shouldn't be listening to this. It's too personal. I turn to go back downstairs. As I do, Justin's phone rings. I stop.

"Oh my god, it's them! I'll put it on speaker."

"Steady," says Atif, with a smile in his voice. "What are you going to be like when the baby's actually born?"

"A nervous wreck," says Justin, sounding deadly serious.

"No, you're not, you're going to be the best," Atif tells him. "The best dad ever."

"Hello? Laura?" Justin says anxiously into the phone.

"It's all fine. Your baby's fine," says Mum's voice. "It's just that I'm going to need to stay in for a couple of nights. Well, at least a couple of nights. You should come in now, is that all right? We can talk about everything then."

"Of course," says Justin hurriedly. "We'll be there as quick as we can. We're on our way."

"Hold on, are the kids okay? I'm going to call Jo in a sec to see if she can stay with them for a bit."

"They're fine," says Atif reassuringly. "Jo's downstairs with them." He doesn't mention all the other people also hanging around in our house.

"And, one more thing, I haven't even got a bag ready yet. I'll text Jo with a list of what I need. Bells can help her find the right stuff. Any chance you could bring that with you?"

Why Bells and not me? I think.

"Of course, anything you need," says Justin. "So… you're definitely not in labour yet? We won't miss the birth, will we?"

"No, definitely not." Mum's voice is calm. "The doctors want to make sure this baby stays safely inside for as long as possible. That's why they're keeping me in. Even another week would make all the difference – give your little one a bit more time to grow. It's nothing to worry about, just one of those things."

I have heard all I need to. I reverse slowly down the stairs, making sure I'm back in the kitchen before Justin and Atif finish the call and come down. So Mum's not coming home, not today, not tomorrow, who knows when? When they come into the kitchen, looking for Auntie Jo, I quietly slip out again. There's so much going on that nobody's paying attention to what I'm doing.

I shut my bedroom door behind me and lean back against it for a moment, simply absorbing the quiet. Then I peel off my jumper and flop down onto my bed. Mum's not here to tell me to get changed first, or to remind me not to leave my muddy clothes in a pile on the floor.

My head is full. It's spinning with images from today: of Auntie Jo's delight as I reach the finish; of standing with Justin in the car park watching Mum and Dad drive away; of Will with Jen Thomas – I can imagine them laughing together like they were at the play. Of Jack red-in-the-face from running – doing something he hates because he cares about me. Of the peace that I felt during the race – like it was just me and the hills. But it's as if I'm looking at all of these images from a distance, like they are happening to someone else instead of me, I'm moving further and further away. I close my eyes, just briefly. And then…

"Ow, get off!"

There's something heavy pressing down on me. I

gradually work out that it's Bells, and that she's sitting on my feet. I shout at her, and she shuffles along the bed.

"What are you doing in my room?" I ask.

"I knocked, honest, but you didn't answer so I came in. Lily and I looked in earlier, but you were asleep, so we left you. But now you've got to get up."

I sit up hastily, rubbing my eyes. I feel a bit sick from all the cake I ate earlier. I've no idea what time it is.

"Where's Lily now?" I ask, looking round anxiously.

"She went home ages ago."

"Good, I don't like the thought of Lily watching me sleep. It's creepy."

"Why are you always so mean about Lily?" asks Bells.

"I'm not mean about her," I protest. "She just always seems to be hanging around."

"Does she annoy you because you actually really like her? You could just ask her out, you know."

"I don't *want* to ask her out."

"Why not?"

I go through in my mind all the many reasons why I would not want to ask Lily out, looking for the most suitable one. I don't feel at my sharpest right now.

"She's only in Year Seven."

"So?"

"I'm in Year Nine."

"So?"

The events of today filter slowly back into my sleepy mind. I don't really understand why Bells and I are having this weird conversation about Lily now, when there's much more important things I need to know.

"Never mind. Where is everyone? What's happening?"

"Mum and Dad are still at the hospital. Justin and Atif have gone there too, but then they're going back to London to get their stuff so they can stay up here till the baby's born…"

"What?" I interrupt. "Like for five weeks? That's crazy. What about their jobs?"

"It's not going to be five weeks. Probably more like a few days." Bells loves knowing what's going on, when I don't. Even more than that, she loves explaining it to me like she's the expert.

"But isn't that too early?"

"Daisy and Evie were early, and they were okay."

"But *this* early?"

Bells shrugs. "Dunno. Anyway, apparently she needs to be on bed rest and special drugs and stuff to stop the baby coming before it's more ready. So Auntie Jo's in charge of us. Everyone else has gone. Go on, get up. We're getting tea on. Dad'll be back in a bit."

I stretch and yawn. "Okay, I'm coming."

"Wait," says Bells. "The back of your hair's all sticking out." I quickly smooth it down.

"Okay now?"

"Yeah."

She's almost out of the door before I ask, "Bells, are you worried about Mum?"

She looks back at me, confused, like I've asked her something totally ridiculous. "Worried about Mum? No, Mum will be fine. Mum's always fine. Nothing bad's going to happen to her."

Bells sounds so certain. She's right – it's hard to imagine Mum being anything other than fine. I can't really remember her ever being ill. Even when we've all had coughs and colds and sickness bugs, Mum always seems to power through at a hundred miles an hour with five times the amount of energy of anyone else. Mum's unstoppable. So the thought of her stuck in a hospital bed is pretty weird.

"I bet she'll hate it in hospital if they won't let her do anything," I say.

"She'll make friends with all the other patients, won't she? Find out everything about..." Bells stops. "Ade, what's that?"

"What?"

"Under your bed, that pink box?"

I look at where she's pointing. Oh god, it's still there. I've stopped noticing it. I keep forgetting to take it back to Jack's mum. I'll do it tomorrow.

"Er…it's Jack's mum's foot spa," I say, like this is the most normal thing in the world to have stashed under my bed. Bells raises her eyebrows at me. "It's like a bath for your feet, I think…" I tail off.

Bells stares at me, hard. "You need more than a bath for your feet. You're still filthy and you haven't even changed out of your kit. I'm not coming anywhere near you unless you have a shower before tea."

"I'm hardly going to have a chance to miss Mum bossing me about, what with you around," I grumble under my breath.

"What? *You* boss me about much more than I boss you. Anyway, I'm not bossy, I've got management skills. Girls are always being told they're bossy, when actually they're just being assertive."

"Okay, you win," I say wearily. I'm not in the mood to argue with Bells. Her management skills are too good. "Now let me alone while I have a shower."

"See you downstairs," she says, smiling broadly at me. Then she pauses for a second. "Your race today, you weren't bad, you know." This is high praise from Bells. "It even looked kind of fun."

"Really? Do you reckon? There's always open days for beginners. You could come along and try it out one time."

I quite like the thought of Bells as a runner. She'll take a while to get up to standard, of course, but then, I could show her the ropes. It could be something we did together, instead of everyone thinking I'm the weird one for spending my weekends running through the mud. She's definitely tough enough.

"Nah," she says, wrinkling up her nose. "Fun for you, not fun for me. Sorry."

There's a noise from downstairs as the front door opens and slams shut again. Dad's home.

Chapter Fourteen

"Thanks, Jo," says Dad, in between mouthfuls of spaghetti bolognese. "Having you around today has been a lifesaver. Hope the kids haven't been playing up for you."

"Course we haven't," says Bells indignantly. "Anyway, Aidan and I are hardly kids, are we?"

"It's my pleasure," says Jo. "You know I'm always around if you need me. How long are they keeping her in for?"

"At least the next couple of days. It's not bad timing actually. I'm not on shift again till Wednesday, should give us time to sort things out a bit. I'll see if I can swap the next shift too." He turns to Chloe and the twins. "I've got special bedtime kisses to pass on from Mum tonight when I read you your stories. She gave them to me before I left the hospital. And I reckon you can all come and visit her after school tomorrow for a top up of kisses, how does that sound?"

Daisy nods. "Evie and me are doing her a picture. She can put it up by her bed."

"What a lovely idea," says Auntie Jo.

Chloe looks up. She's feeding Toto bits of her tea under the table when she thinks no one's looking. "Can Toto come and visit her too? I bet she'd cheer Mum up."

"Not in the hospital!" says Bells. "Don't be daft, you can't take a dog in."

"'Fraid not, Chloe. Bells is right," says Dad. "However, we do need to remember to walk Toto every day while Mum's in hospital." He rubs his face with his hands. "There's such a *lot* to remember. She's given me a list."

Evie looks up from scraping her spaghetti all onto one side of her plate, so none of it is touching the sauce. "We can put Toto in our picture," she tells Chloe. "Then Mum can still see her."

"I still don't get why she has to stay in hospital if she's not actually having the baby," I say. "I mean, if she needs to rest, can't she rest at home? We can look after her here."

"Can you imagine your mum resting at home? She'd be trying to get up on her feet in no time," says Dad. "No, they'll both be safe in hospital." For a moment, I wonder who he means by "both", when I've just been talking about Mum. Oh, of course, it's the baby.

"They need to keep an eye on the baby so it's not born too early, and to make sure that neither of them get an infection," continues Dad. "It's the best place for them."

"I'll head home after tea, if you don't need me for anything else," says Auntie Jo, starting to stack up the plates. "I'll call tomorrow, see what the news is. I've got a hectic week at work so I want to try and get ahead of myself tonight, especially as I'm not in on Friday."

I'm not really paying attention. Instead I'm thinking about all the things that Mum would normally remind us about that now we need to remember. I'm just hoping there's some clean school uniform somewhere. "Friday?" I ask.

"Yeah, I'm getting the train down to London on Friday, picking up my race number, then catching up with a few friends I haven't seen for ages on Saturday. I'm staying at their place. Won't be a late one though, not with the big race the morning after."

"So when are Bells and I going down? Aren't we all going together?" I realize that we still haven't talked about exactly when we'll be with Justin and Atif over the marathon and how we're getting to their flat.

There's an awkward silence. All I can hear is Daisy's fork scraping up the last of the sauce on her plate.

Then Dad and Auntie Jo both start talking at once.

"Well, I don't know, but..." she says, just as he says, "I think plans are going to have to change..."

They both stop, exchange glances, then Dad says quietly, "I'm sorry, Aidan, and you too, Bells, but it's just not going to be possible. Not now. Justin and Atif'll be here anyway, up in Sheffield with us. We can watch the marathon on TV instead, can't we?"

The disappointment builds up inside me, making my stomach go cold. Not all at once, but gradually creeping up, like stepping into freezing water, where you lose feeling step by step.

I know what I *want* to say. I want to shout and scream and storm out and slam doors. I want to say how unfair it is and how everything is Justin and Atif's fault and why did Mum agree to have their stupid baby in the first place and what about me, me, me? But I don't.

I know what I *should* say too – that it's okay, I understand, sometimes things don't go to plan, it's not the end of the world, the most important thing is being here for Mum. But I don't say any of that either.

I just sit there, like I'm under the water, like I've gone numb.

Auntie Jo's swaying from one foot to the other, glancing anxiously at Dad. "Perhaps I shouldn't go to London either. Family's more important than just some race. What if you need me here?"

"It's not 'just some race'!" I protest, finding my voice again.

"Don't be daft," says Dad. He looks genuinely shocked. "None of us would ever forgive ourselves if you didn't run next weekend. Not after all that work and all that money you raised. Your big sister would have something to say about that if you didn't go because of her. We'll be fine here, won't we, kids? After all, we're Team Taylor, aren't we?"

I force myself to smile. The girls all nod and Daisy and Evie both try to climb onto Dad's lap at once. Toto knows something's going on; she rests her chin on Chloe's lap and wags her tail madly.

The rest of the evening is manic. I don't really have time to think. Which is good, as I'm trying not to. I don't want to let the disappointment about the marathon creep up on me again, so I just stay busy. The twins are tired out from this morning, still wired on cake and obviously finding it strange without Mum. Even with Dad's extra kisses and stories, they whine about going to bed, while Bells, Chloe and I all race to get in the bathroom first and accuse each other of moving the homework we've each left lying around and now can't find.

I thought I'd be wide awake after sleeping for so long this afternoon, but I'm tired again. I want to sleep so I can get through tonight and then tomorrow at school, so I can see for myself if Mum really is okay. I don't want to rely on what anyone else tells me or thinks that I need to know. Mum will tell it like it is. Maybe it won't be so bad in the morning, maybe the hospital will change their mind and send her home, and maybe I'll be able to go to the marathon after all.

I turn off my light and curl up under the duvet. I'm drifting off to sleep when my phone buzzes. I almost can't be bothered to check it. But then I do. It's a goodnight text from Mum, sending me love, saying well done for the race and wishing me sweet dreams. I smile to myself. It's not as good as a hug, but it'll do. I usually shrug her off, or moan, or ask her to give me some space when she tries to hug me now, but Mum still has the best hugs ever. They make you feel safe, like nothing and no one can reach you. She's looked after loads of kids and I bet every single one of them remembers what it's like getting one of her hugs.

I'm just about to reply when there's another buzz. This text is a bulleted list of what I need to remember for school tomorrow, what Mum wants me to buy on the way home using the spare cash from the jar in the kitchen. And a reminder to put my muddy kit in the wash before going to bed. I turn off my phone and burrow back down under the duvet. That was an even better goodnight message. Nothing's too wrong with Mum if she's still taking charge of all of us even from her hospital bed. I yawn and stretch. I'm almost asleep. I'll sort out my kit in the morning.

Chapter Fifteen

I hate hospitals. The echoey corridors and the plasticky floors that make your shoes squeak. The tatty posters and the smell of hand sanitizer and the way that even things that people try to make look cheerful, still look depressing. And there's people everywhere – visitors, patients, staff. Everyone can hear what you're saying. At any minute a doctor or a nurse could open the door or pull back the curtains, nothing's really private.

It's our third visit now, after school on Monday and every day since. Each one is pretty quick, as there are only a couple of hours between the end of school and the end of visiting time. It's probably a good thing so we don't tire Mum out. No one else in the antenatal ward has nearly as many visitors as she does. On Monday, Mum explained how everyone in the ward has some complication with their pregnancy. She says she's already seen loads of people come and go while she's been stuck in bed.

"So these are your husband and kids?" asks the woman in the bed next to Mum in a loud whisper as we walk in with Dad. I don't recognize her from yesterday. She must be new. "My husband'll be here in a minute too."

"Yes, that's my Pete," Mum tells her. "Pete, this is Janie, my new neighbour. And, well, it'll take me most of visiting time to introduce everyone, but they're all mine!" We take it in turns to reach down to give Mum a kiss or a hug. Daisy clambers up next to her on the bed even though she's not supposed to.

Dad nods and smiles at Janie, as she looks questioningly at us. We're probably the most excitement she's had all day. "You've got quite a brood there already, love. Going to be rushed off your feet with a new baby too, aren't you? So, what are you having – number six?" She doesn't wait for an answer, just keeps on talking. "This one's only my second and that feels like enough to cope with. My husband's a teacher – I mean, that's great in the holidays but in term-time it's so inflexible. I've had to get my mum in to help with my little girl while I'm in here. She's so excited about being a big sister!" She turns to us. "Hope all you girls are going to be helping Mummy out with the housework when she gets home with the baby."

"It's not just girls that should help out," mutters Bells crossly under her breath.

"Well, actually, I'm not going to need that much help..." replies Mum brightly and my heart sinks.

"I'll go and find some chairs, shall I?" I interrupt, trying to distract her.

"Oh, thanks, Aidan, love." She turns back to the woman in the next bed. "Actually, I'm a surrogate. I'm having this baby for a friend, so it'll go straight to its real parents after the birth."

"Oh," says Janie, struggling to find the right words. "Oh, I see." Except I'm not sure that she does. She pauses and lowers her voice to a whisper again. "Is that legal?"

Mum laughs. "Last time I checked! It's much more common than you'd think."

"Goodness, so your friend, she can't have her own baby, medical reasons I suppose..." Janie continues thoughtfully. "Well, what an amazing thing to do for another woman, that's real sisterhood. I swear I couldn't do it. Give my baby away like that."

I drag a couple of blue plastic chairs over from the corner of the room; they make a horrible scraping sound across the floor. But even the noise isn't enough to stop Mum now that she's got going.

"I suppose so," says Mum. "My friend, *him* and his husband…" She stresses the word "him" in a way which makes me think she's enjoying making Janie's eyebrows shoot up. "They'll make smashing parents. I'll introduce you later when they come in to visit."

"Well, I'd better not disturb you no more," says Janie abruptly, picking up her phone. "You'll be wanting to spend time with your family."

Mum turns to us. "So, how is everyone? I hope you've got some good stories for me. I'm bored out of my mind in here. I've read all the mags that Justin brought in yesterday, and I've done all the sudokus, even the extra hard one."

"Yeah, I have, me first," says Bells straight away. "Oh my god, Mum, you won't believe what we had to do in Science today. It was disgusting, but kind of cool too. We had to cut up these pigs' kidneys and they were all squelchy and gross, and then we had to draw them. Then Ollie Hart told Lily that it looked like her face, just to wind her up, so she threatened to throw it at him. That shut him up."

"She wouldn't have done it though, would she?" asks Chloe anxiously. "Not really."

"Maybe she would," says Bells. "She didn't this time cos Ms Martin came over. Don't think Ollie will dare say anything like that to Lily again though."

"Poor pigs," says Chloe sadly. "I bet they don't want to be cut up."

I can't help notice that Janie in the next bed looks up from her phone at this to shoot us a disapproving look.

"That sounds like a bit of drama, Bells," says Mum, her eyes ranging over all of us as she talks. "Chloe, just bend down here a sec, let's smarten you up." Chloe leans in and Mum deftly straightens her ponytail for her. "Did you even brush your hair this morning?"

Chloe looks away. "Maybe."

"Goodness, Laura," says Dad. "The amount of hair-brushing and plaiting that needs doing every day in this family. It's a nightmare to keep up now there's only me on the team at home. I blame all these girls with their long hair." He sounds quite cheerful about it though. "I think I've done an all right job, considering."

"I think you have too," says Mum smiling. "I can't wait to be back with you all though."

"It's not just girls that have long hair," says Bells. "That's sexist. Boys can have long hair too, you know."

"True," says Dad. "But it just so happens there are no long-haired boys in our house, running around with unbrushed hair looking for lost hairbands just before it's time for school."

"So, how's Toto?" asks Mum.

"Fine," I say. "Dad's been taking her for walks, and when he's back on shift tomorrow, I can get up early and take her before school."

"On shift tomorrow?" asks Mum. "I thought you were going to change that?"

"I'm trying," says Dad. "But we're so understaffed at the moment. I've definitely got early next week off though, it's just the next few days that could be tricky. But, of course, if you go into labour, then they'll just have to manage without me. I'll talk to Jo and Jack's mum has offered to help out where she can – we'll sort something out, don't worry."

Bells eyes go wide. At first, I think it's because she's worried about how we'll manage when Dad's back at work, then I look behind me.

A tall, dark-haired man has just come into the ward and is striding towards us. He's so familiar, but at first I can't work out who he is. Then I realize it's because he looks different from usual. No tracksuit. No whistle. And what on earth is he doing here? I hastily, and instinctively, tuck in my school shirt and sit up straighter. Then Mr Evans stops at Janie's bed.

This is awkward. It's weird to think of teachers having real lives outside of school. Especially teachers like Mr Evans. I don't like the thought of him – or any of my teachers – overhearing all our private stuff. I slump down low in my seat, in the hope he won't notice me, but Bells has a better idea.

"I'll just pull the curtains round, shall I, Mum?" And she leaps up to draw them across between the two beds.

Bells talks more about her day at school, but in a quieter voice than usual, I guess because she doesn't want Mr Evans to overhear some of her comments. Mum tells a story to the twins. Dad passes on hellos from some of the families that Mum normally child-minds for.

"You look tired," says Dad finally.

"Charming!" says Mum.

"I meant, we'd better get going, let you get some rest before Justin and Atif get here. I need to get this lot home anyway."

We hug Mum goodbye and then walk past Janie's bed on our way out. Her and Mr Evans's heads are close together, talking. She pauses, looks up and nods over at us meaningfully. I guess she's been telling him all the juicy details about our family. Mr Evans follows her gaze and looks surprised when he recognizes our blazers. He stares at our faces for a moment.

"Hello, Aidan," he says stiffly. "And, er, Imogen?"

"It's Isabella, Bells, 7P," says Bells.

There's an awkward silence.

"Oh yes, of course, Isabella. Well, see you both at school tomorrow."

"Yes, Mr Evans," says Bells, but before she's finished speaking, he's turned back to his wife, their heads together again.

Just before we reach the automatic exit doors – the ones which Daisy and Evie love running through again and again to make them whoosh open and shut – Dad spots Justin and Atif sitting on a couple of those plastic chairs which are bolted to the floor.

"Hello, fellas," says Dad. "How are you? We've just seen Laura, she's in good form. She'll love to see you." He sits down next to Atif, stretching out his long legs. "Oh, you're not drinking that disgusting coffee from the café bar, are you?"

"Afraid so," says Atif. "Guess we'd better get used to it."

"Do you think we should wait a few minutes before going up?" asks Justin. "Give her a chance to have a break?"

"Good idea," says Dad. "Happy for us to stick around with you? I'd like to catch up on a couple of things."

Justin's eyes open wider.

"Everything's fine," Dad reassures him. "Honestly. The baby's still healthy, hanging on inside like a trooper. Here, Aidan." He gets a note out of his wallet and hands it to me. "Could you get me a cup of that horrible coffee? I guess it can't be much worse than the stuff we make at the fire station, and I can drink gallons of that. Maybe a couple of packets of crisps as well. Take the others with you. Tell Daisy and Evie they can choose the flavours. But no more salt-and-vinegar. I'm fed up of the smell of those."

I'm torn. I want to go to the café so that I don't have to hang around small-talking with Justin and Atif, but I don't want to miss out on hearing anything Dad has to say either. He and Mum always tell us everything, sometimes even things I'd rather not know, but maybe it's different now. Maybe there are things they're telling Justin and Atif, because they are the baby's parents, but not telling us. Maybe Dad wants us out of the way.

When we come back from the café with Dad's coffee, packets of cheese-and-onion crisps, and a cheeky packet of Minstrels that I threw in at the last minute, I think my suspicions might be right.

"It could work…" I hear Justin say as we get closer.

"Actually, it would work really well. We'd love it. But are you sure you don't mind?" adds Atif.

"Mind?" says Dad. "Why would I mind? It would be ideal for all of us. It's just for a few days, the girls'll love it too. And, Aidan, well, he'll be okay."

"What are you talking about?" I ask. "What will I be okay about?"

"Thanks, Ade," says Dad, as I pass him the paper cup of muddy brown liquid. "You were quick." He takes a sip of coffee and grimaces, then rips open and pours in three little packs of sugar one by one. Stirs. Sips again. "That's better. Well, while you were off getting these, we've come up with an idea. Girls, how would you feel about Justin and Atif coming to stay at our house for a few days?"

"Like a sleepover?" says Bells. "Sure, that would be cool."

"Please, please, please come," says Daisy. "You can read us stories at bedtime." Justin and Atif exchange looks.

"Course we can. You can show us all your favourite books," says Atif. "I love stories, especially animal stories. I hope you've got lots of animal stories."

"And will you make us hot chocolate?" says Chloe. "Auntie Jo always makes us hot chocolate with marshmallows when she babysits."

"Does she now?" says Dad. "So that's what our children get up to when we're not around!"

"I think we can run to hot chocolate, maybe even marshmallows too," says Justin, grinning in a bemused way, like he's not quite sure how he got himself into this.

"What?" I say through gritted teeth, turning my back on Justin and Atif a little, and talking only to Dad. "Do you mean *they* are going to be looking after us while you're on shift and Mum's in hospital? This is your plan? I thought you were going to talk to Auntie Jo or Jack's mum or, I don't know, *anyone* else would be better."

Atif leans forward. "Pete, maybe we should give this a bit more thought. We don't want to cause any trouble for you."

"Nonsense," says Dad. "It's no trouble at all. Like I said, you'll be helping us out."

He stands up. "Need a bit more sugar in this coffee. Show me where you got it from, Aidan." And he steers me by the elbow, away from Justin and Atif, who are facing a barrage of excited questions from the twins and Chloe.

"Come on, Ade, don't be like this," Dad says under his breath. "It's perfect. It would be a lot to ask Jack's mum – looking after the five of you – and Jo's going to be off to London on Friday..."

"Yeah, like I could forget that!" I interrupt sulkily.

I glance over my shoulder. Atif's engrossed in something my sisters are telling him, but Justin's not. He's looking over at me and Dad with a worried expression on his face.

"But Justin and Atif... They want to stay in Sheffield till the birth now anyway," continues Dad. "They can still work up here. It's all emails and online meetings from what I can tell – that's just as easy from our house as anywhere else. They can stay in mine and Mum's room while she's at the hospital and I'm at the fire station, and work on their laptops from our kitchen table while you're at school. They'd booked themselves into a hotel, would you believe? Didn't want to put Jo out any more than they have already. Well, we can't have them worrying about that. This is much better, and it'll be like a crash course in parenting for them – looking after you lot!" He laughs.

"I don't *need* looking after," I say. "None of us does."

"Really?"

"I mean, *I* can look after the girls. It's only a couple of days."

"Aidan, I can't leave a 13-year-old boy in charge of four other kids, don't be daft. They'd have social services on me like a shot."

"But it's okay to leave all of us with two virtual strangers?"

"How many times, Aidan? They are *not* strangers. They are our friends. You didn't mind the idea of going to stay with them in London, did you? This isn't any different."

He's right, I didn't mind that. Not once I'd got used to the idea. Not if it meant going to London, and watching the marathon and, yeah okay, having a bit of snoop round their fancy flat. But this is different. Justin and Atif in our house, staying in Mum and Dad's room, like *they've* become our parents. It just feels wrong.

"I need you," he says softly. "You're the oldest. I need

you to set an example for the others, to be strong for them. I know it's strange and unsettling right now, but that won't last for ever. Just for a few days. We'll be back to normal soon. I need you just to do this one thing. I'm just trying to do my best, for all of us, and I'm relying on you, son. I need you on the team – one hundred per cent."

I nod. Just a tiny nod but enough for Dad to see. Okay. Just this one thing. I can do this for Mum and Dad. I've got to. I don't want to make things harder for them by acting like a spoiled child.

We walk back over to the others.

"Well, that's settled then," says Dad. "See you tomorrow morning, with all your stuff. You'd better go up now. See Laura before she wonders where you've got to."

"Thanks," says Justin. His voice sounds a bit wobbly. "Not just for this. I mean, for all of it. The way you've welcomed us into your family. You didn't have to do that. It means everything. And knowing that in just a few days, we'll have our own little family, it's..." Atif puts a hand on Justin's arm. I look and then look away.

"We're glad to," says Dad warmly. "Both of us are."

Well, I think, that's all right for him to say. What about Mum? She's the one stuck upstairs in a hospital bed. That's even before giving birth, which sounds pretty unpleasant to me.

"Oh," Dad says, turning to Bells and me. "There he is again. That bloke who knew you earlier." I turn and see Mr Evans striding through the automatic doors. He doesn't see us. "One of your teachers, is it?"

"Yeah," says Bells, making a face. "It's Mr Evans. We have him for PE. He's awful, really shouty. And he never pays any attention to the girls, he can't even get our names right. He's only interested in the boys, those that are good enough for the teams anyway."

"I'm sure he's not that bad," says Dad absent-mindedly.

"He is!" I say. "I don't have him now but I had him in Year Seven. Jack does though. He always picks on Jack. I heard that he, well, anyway, it was pretty bad…" I don't really want to go into it now.

"Our Jack?" says Dad, looking thoughtful. "I can see how a lad like Jack might struggle a bit in PE, but that's out of order, I mean for a teacher to pick on *any kid*. Has Jack told anyone about it?"

I shake my head. He might not even have said anything to me if I hadn't been there when Sam and Ethan and the others copied Mr Evans's insults towards him.

"And what about you?" asks Atif, leaning forward. "Have you said anything? Told another teacher about it maybe?"

"No," I say indignantly. You never tell on someone, you just don't. Atif *must* remember that from being at school. He's not *that* old. Although this is different, it's a teacher, not someone else in the class. Maybe I *should* say something. It's probably too late now. And I wasn't even there, was I? Plus, who would believe what I say rather than a teacher?

Atif's looking straight at me. "Maybe you should think about it, Aidan. If he is being picked on, especially if it's by a teacher, then Jack will need his friends. I'm not trying to tell you what to do, but I remember what it's like being at school and being singled out for being different, that's all."

"Yeah, okay," I say, staring down at the floor. "Maybe." I just want Atif to stop looking at me like that, making me feel bad, like it's all my fault.

Great, I think as we say goodbye and finally make our way back to the car. They haven't even moved in yet, and already Atif's starting to act like he thinks he's my dad.

Chapter Sixteen

The last couple of days have been like a kind of limbo. Mum still in hospital. Dad still at work. Going to school. Coming home. Nothing changing. Nothing happening. Nothing except Justin and Atif making themselves at home in our house.

It can't go on like this for much longer. The girls are carrying on like everything's normal. Apart from Bells, I guess they're too little to be worried, but I've been online, reading about everything that could go wrong with Mum. Even if it's low risk, there's still *some* risk, right?

I hate this waiting. I can tell Justin hates it too. He can't keep still. He's like Mum, always moving, always doing something. Put something down for a minute and he'll clear it away, and then wipe underneath where it was.

Atif's more laid back. It's only been a couple of days, but I do feel like I'm getting to know them better, even like them a bit more. That still doesn't mean I'm happy that they're here.

However, I have to admit it does smell good in the kitchen. Kind of spicy and rich, not like the sort of thing that Mum or Dad normally make. I'm starving as usual after a run. I went further today too, pushing myself hard. Trying not to think.

"Aidan, perfect timing," calls Justin from the kitchen. "We're going to eat in a minute. You can always shower after."

I don't say anything. I take a deep breath. I decided on the run, I was going to try harder. For Mum's sake. But still, it's not up to him to tell me when I should or shouldn't shower.

I go into the kitchen. It's warm and cosy. The blinds are drawn even though it's not dark yet, but it is getting dim out there. The sky is stuffed with grey rain clouds, waiting to burst. It's noisy too, and high-pitched, everyone talking and laughing at once.

The kitchen table is covered in bits of coloured paper and glitter and bright bottles of poster paint. Atif sweeps them all up into piles on the kitchen work surface.

"We've been doing craft!" says Daisy excitedly. "Look,

Aidan!" She points at the row of pictures drying on the shelf. Atif leans over with a damp cloth and wipes the paint off her sticky hands as she talks.

"Nice work, Daze," I say. "Where did you get all the stuff from?"

"Oh," says Atif. "I found a whole crate of art bits and pieces in the cupboard. I hope that was all right to use."

"Well, not really," I say. "That's what Mum uses with the kids she looks after. It's her child-minding cupboard. It's not for us, it's for her business."

"Chill out," says Bells. "Mum wouldn't mind. You know we're allowed to use it sometimes. Anyway, we've all been having a good time." She pauses. "Well, we were. Till you got home."

"Oh shut up," I say.

There's an awkward silence, like Bells and I are both waiting for Mum to say, "Be nice to your sister", but she's not here to say it.

Justin looks from Bells to me, takes a breath, and then seems to change his mind about getting involved. Instead, he wipes his hands on his apron. Except it's not his. Across his front it says: *Team Taylor: Captain and Barbecuer-in-Chief.* He's wearing Dad's apron.

"What are you wearing that for? That's not yours," I say. I'm aware that, despite the promises I made to myself not to be like this, I'm sounding like a sulky toddler.

"Come on, let's eat," says Atif quickly. He starts serving up steaming platefuls.

"What's in it?" asks Evie suspiciously.

"It's black bean enchiladas," says Justin. "It's a Mexican dish. It's just like having a veggie wrap with a bit of sauce, Evie."

"It's really good," says Bells.

I'd like to make a point by not eating it, but I'm too hungry to say no. It takes one mouthful to realize that Bells is right. It tastes delicious. If everything had gone to plan, I bet we'd be eating this in Justin and Atif's London flat right now, instead of off mismatched plates round our own kitchen table.

Justin's phone rings. Only for a second, because he's on it like a shot. He mouths "sorry" to Atif and dashes into the hallway with the phone clamped to his ear. He shuts the door behind him. He obviously doesn't want us to listen in on the conversation.

He comes back in after a couple of minutes, leans over to whisper something in Atif's ear, and then carries on eating.

"What?" I ask. "What's going on?"

"It's all fine," says Justin quickly.

"What's all fine?" I ask.

The phone rings again, and Justin repeats his disappearing act.

"What's happening?" I ask Atif again. "Mum and Dad always tell us what's going on."

"Okay," he says, putting down his knife and fork carefully. Everyone's looking at him now. "That was your dad. It's what we expected, the hospital *are* worried that the baby might have an infection, and that it's not safe to wait any longer, so they'll help your mum's labour to start tonight. Justin and I will go in for the birth. Your dad will be there too, to support your mum. He was going to phone Jack's mum to see if she can come round now to look after you tonight while we're at the hospital. I guess that's her on the phone."

"Oh my god, that's so exciting. The baby's coming! Is Mum okay?" asks Bells.

"Of course she is," says Atif.

"Yeah, but is she really?" I say, getting to my feet. I can't stay sitting down. "You said it yourself, she's not safe. I mean, why didn't *she* phone us? Or why didn't Dad? What are you not telling us? It's not fair, passing us around from adult to adult, like no one wants us around, and not even telling us what's really going on."

"It's not like that, Aidan," says Atif. "I know this is a strange time, we're all a bit on edge, but honestly, it's not that people don't want you around, not at all." I stare at him in stony silence. Everyone's stopped eating.

Justin comes back in and sits down like nothing's wrong. He leans across to Evie, who has barely touched her food. She doesn't like it when different foods touch on her plate and everything about this meal is all mixed in together. Mum and Dad know that, but Justin doesn't. Or maybe they told him and he just forgot.

"Come on, Evie, give it a try. It's not so bad, is it? How about I have a bite and then you have a bite? Deal?"

"She doesn't have to eat your food!" I shout, pushing my chair back. "You're not our parents. You can't tell us what to do."

Chloe looks at me wide-eyed.

"Whoa," says Bells, shaking her head at me.

"Now, Aidan," says Atif, like he's making a huge effort to stay calm. "Why don't you just sit down and we'll talk about this? Your parents aren't here, so we're looking after you. We're only here because they asked us to be. Okay?"

All the thoughts and worries that I've been keeping quiet about since Mum went into hospital start to pour out. I can't keep them packed away any more.

"They're not here because Mum's in hospital. And you know whose fault that is? Yours. If she wasn't having your baby, she'd be here with us. If it wasn't for you, she'd be safe."

Suddenly, I can't bear to be in the house any more. There's too many people, too much to think about and worry about, too much that I can't control. I need to get away.

"Stop it," says Justin, his voice rising. He slams his fist on the table. "You can't talk to us like that, Aidan. You need to apologize right now."

"I can talk however I like, it's my house not yours," I shout back, pushing past Bells and out of the kitchen, desperate to escape. As I go, my arm brushes against the pile on the work surface, sending it toppling over. Paint bottles slam onto the floor and roll away, and a cloud of glitter and shredded tissue paper rises up into the air before starting to settle on the table. Daisy giggles nervously as a strip of paper lands in the middle of her plate.

I throw myself through the front door and slam it as loud as I can behind me. It doesn't make me feel any better.

I think I can hear Atif shouting my name as the door bangs shut, but I don't stick around to listen. I start running without knowing where I'm going. Just putting one foot in front of the other, while I work out where I can go to get away from here.

I run up the hill past Jack's house. The lights are on inside. I could go in, but I'm not ready to see anybody yet, not even Jack. I don't think I'd want to explain to him what happened either, what I said and did. Jack's my best friend, he knows me so well, he'd be on my side, but…

If Auntie Jo were in Sheffield right now, I'd go straight to her flat, no question. She'd let me in without asking anything awkward or annoying. Well, at least, not at first. She'd just let me be. Till I was ready. But she's in London, staying with her friends, getting psyched up for tomorrow's race. So I can't go there.

Unless…but it's a ridiculous idea. I *could* go down to London. It's not *that* late, I could get a train and I could call Auntie Jo when I get there. I'm sure her friends could squeeze me in. I'd be no trouble. Then there'd be no more having to play happy families with Justin and Atif. Actually, I bet they'd be pleased to have me out of the way. And I'd get to see the marathon.

I'd call Mum and Dad and let them know where I was, I'm not totally irresponsible. They'd be cross, but with all the excitement about the baby, they'd get over it. And it would be worth it. Except…what about Mum in hospital? What if I made things worse? What if I already have?

Perhaps I should run to the hospital instead. Then I could see if Mum's all right. I can remember my way up to the ward. Unless they've moved her now. And what if they wouldn't let me in? I could ring first. No, maybe it's better just to turn up.

I reach for my phone. Then realize that I've been wasting my time in thinking about any of this. I have *nothing* with me, nothing, no phone, no money, no keys to get back in the house, not even a jumper. Just my running clothes from earlier and that's all. I left in too much of a hurry. I am the most useless, ill-prepared runaway ever.

I'm zigzagging through the streets now, not paying much attention to which way I turn. It doesn't matter anyway – I'm not going *to* anywhere, I'm just going *away*. It's quiet out. I guess most people are inside having their tea. A couple of runners come the other way. They break their chat to nod hello to me as they go past.

I slow down – my feet have taken me a strange roundabout route, but have eventually brought me to the Field, just a few minutes away from home. I might as well stop here and get my breath back, think about what to do next. I sit on the big flat rock and look out over Sheffield.

There's still enough daylight to make out the buildings and the roads, but lights are starting to come on all over the city. I can't focus my thoughts on anything, especially not on what I'm going to do next.

I don't know how long I sit there, staring at the city, before I sense someone behind me. Well, more than sense. I can hear his heavy, laboured breathing, like he's not used to running but has been doing it anyway. I stiffen. Before I can look round or get to my feet and carry on running, he sits down beside me on the rock.

"Not a bad view," he says breathlessly. "I can see why you'd want to spend time up here. It's a good place to think, right?"

Chapter Seventeen

I continue to stare out over the city rather than turn to look at Atif next to me.

"How…?" I ask finally.

"How did I find you? It wasn't that hard. I went to Jack's. He told me you liked it up here. He wanted to come with me, help track you down, but I didn't want to risk taking him on a wild goose chase round Sheffield if you didn't turn out to be here. Although I probably should have done, he knows the city a whole lot better than I do." He pauses. "Look, I'm just going to text Justin, okay? Let him know everything's fine. That's all."

"Okay," I say.

He sends his text and then we sit in silence. He doesn't ask me anything else. Atif's very good at just sitting and waiting.

"Look," I say at last, pointing. "There's the university, and the stadium. Then, closer, you can see our house." Atif nods. "And over there, it's the hospital."

I wonder whether Mum's looking out of her window down there. I hope she is. Even if she can only see as far as the hospital car park, it feels like a connection somehow. I wonder what Atif's thinking when he looks at the hospital. Is he thinking that's where his baby's just about to be born? He must be really nervous, dying to be there, yet instead he's sitting here with me.

"I hope the baby's okay," I say suddenly.

"Thanks. I think it will be fine. Twelve per cent of babies are born more than a month before their due date, and ninety-five per cent of those don't need to go into special care when they're born. The numbers are in our favour."

I look at him in surprise. I wasn't expecting him to reel off percentages at me. He gives me an embarrassed smile.

"What can I say? I work in insurance. And I like information, it helps me feel like things are under control..."

"Even when they're not?" I ask.

"*Especially* when they're not! Anyway, nothing's ever totally under control, is it? I hate to say it, but unexpected things do happen. They always will. Nothing stays the same for ever."

We sit in silence for a bit longer. I'm glad. There's too much going on in my head to want to talk right now. I listen to the crows squawking above our heads and the faint rush of traffic in the distance.

"Is *that* why you don't like us?" Atif says. It's a question, not an accusation. "Is it because we've burst into your life, into your family, and set all these changes in motion when you weren't ready for them?"

"It's not that I don't like you and Justin…" I say, but then I remember all the times in the last year when I've acted like I don't. When I've left rooms as they've come in and made excuses not to be around when they were coming, when I've refused to laugh at their jokes – even when they were funny – or to acknowledge all the kind things they've done. And then there are the things I said and did tonight. I feel as if Atif can see right into my head.

"It's okay, Aidan, it's a bit late for politeness now. You don't *have* to like us. We can take it. But, and I should have said this right at the start, we're going to be around for a while, so it would be easier if we tried to get along, don't you think?"

"Yeah, I s'pose," I say, feeling like some spoiled little kid.

"Is that the only reason?" he asks. "It's not anything to do with us being gay, is it?"

"No," I burst out. "Of course not."

"It's just, I've noticed, sometimes, you seem uncomfortable just being near us. I'm sure it's not obvious to anyone else. It's just you learn to pick up on these things."

My face is burning.

"How did you know you were gay?" I find myself asking. "I mean, at first?"

Atif shoots a look at me. He looks like he's trying to work out where that question came from.

He sighs. "Well, if you ask Justin, he'd say that he always knew. Or at least, ever since he was little, he knew he was different. That, and a childhood obsession with the bloke who presented Blue Peter, back when we were kids. I'm still not sure he's totally got over that one." He smiles. "But it wasn't quite like that with me. I was older. And even when it was clear to me that I wasn't interested in girls, I still didn't think I could be gay."

"Why not?" I'm so hooked on what he's saying that I've forgotten to be embarrassed about asking questions.

"Because in most of the media when I was younger, you'd only see white people who were visibly out and proud. People that looked like me weren't gay, and certainly you wouldn't see Muslims proudly declaring that they're gay. You know, with my parents, we speak to each other in Urdu. Even just finding the words in Urdu to explain what it meant to be a member of the LGBT community was really hard."

"So what do your family think about you now?"

Atif laughs. "We managed to talk about it, eventually, and we discovered that often it worked better *not* to spell everything out. It was awkward and difficult to begin with, but now we're fine, we've learnt from each other. And they absolutely adore Justin. They think he's a good match for me. He's so polite, you know. It's him, not me, who remembers to send my mum a card on her birthday and at Eid, and he always compliments her on her cooking."

"And what about the baby?"

"My mum can't wait for another grandchild. My two big sisters are well ahead of me on that score though, so she's already got six."

"You've got sisters?" I realize that in all the weeks and months that we've known Justin and Atif, I've barely considered their families or their lives away from us. I've never asked them anything before. And yet they know our family inside out.

"Just like you, Aidan, I'm the only boy. I feel your pain." I risk looking up at him and he grins at me. I grin back, just a little bit.

"And could people tell?" I ask. "I mean, did they know

before you told them? Were there, I don't know, signs they spotted or something?"

"Oh, I don't know, some people did, I suppose. It's so long since being gay has felt like a secret for me, something that people would need to guess. It's just one part of my life…" He stops talking as a black and white collie streaks past us at top speed, followed by its much slower owner.

When he starts talking again, his voice is quieter, more serious. "Aidan, are we still talking about me and Justin? Are you sure we're not talking about someone else?"

Oh my god, he knows, he knows, he's always known. It must be so obvious.

I swallow. This is it. "What do you mean?"

"Jack," he says. "Are you trying to tell me something about Jack? It's okay, you can trust me, I won't give away any secrets."

"Jack?" I am so surprised. It's not like Atif even knows Jack that well, although they do get on when they're both round our house. "Jack's not gay. He told me he wasn't."

"Oh," says Atif. "Your mum thought…"

"Mum talked to you about Jack?" This was getting even weirder.

"She asked us if we thought Jack was gay. She was worried that he might be having a hard time about it at school, and hoped that he'd be able to talk to us if he needed to, you know, as people who might understand what he was going through. She really sees him as part of your extended family, doesn't she? Well, you all do." He looks into the distance. More lights keep appearing across the city skyline. "Seeing that openness was one of the things that made me think she'd be the perfect person to be a surrogate for us, that maybe there'd be room for us in that wider family too."

"You didn't talk to Jack though?"

"The time was never quite right. Although I wish I had. When you said about that teacher picking on him, it made me wonder if your mum was right."

"I think he would've talked to you, if he needed to. Actually, a few months ago, he told *me* that *I* should, that you'd understand."

"Okay," says Atif carefully, waiting for me to explain.

"I told Jack I was gay," I say in a rush. "He asked and I said yes. And then I said no – that I was just joking. And since then, we haven't talked about it at all. He wanted to talk about it, but I didn't."

He waits for me to carry on. When it's clear that I've finished talking, he says, "And now? What would you say now? Yes, or no, or something else? And, by the way, Aidan, any of those answers is absolutely fine."

"I wouldn't say no," I say slowly. "But I don't know.

How could I say yes when I'm not sure?"

"You don't have to be sure. And you don't have to use a label because other people want you to. You don't have to be like anyone else. You just have to be you, and at some point you have to be brave enough to let other people see who that person really is."

"It's just…" I start, knowing what I'm about to say will sound stupid. "I'm not into all the things that you're supposed to be into, I mean, if you're gay."

"Like what?" says Atif. He doesn't sound like he's laughing at me – yet – so I carry on.

"I don't know." I do know, exactly, but I can't express it. "Like on *Queer Eye*, where they're all so well-dressed and loud and over-the-top and all air-kissing and stuff. That's more like Jack, it's not like me. And I'm into sport. Like, can you be gay and into sport?"

Something has shifted. A few minutes ago I would have done anything to avoid talking about this with anyone, let alone Atif or Justin. Now I just feel relief at finally being able to ask some of my questions out loud. How did I not notice before what a good listener Atif is?

"Of course you can be gay and into sport," says Atif. "That's as ridiculous as me thinking I couldn't be gay because I was Muslim. There have been gay athletes who have won Olympic medals, you know. Top of their game.

You can be absolutely anything you want to be, Aidan. Being gay's just one part of who you are."

We sit there for a bit longer. I feel like if I said something now, it would break the spell.

"If it helps, I'm pretty sure your mum and dad would be cool with it, with whatever."

As he says the words, I know for sure that's true. Right down deep inside, nothing could be more true than that. So what am I so afraid of? I know what.

"Yeah, Mum and Dad. But what about school? If you stand out, you get picked on. It's not just Jack it happens to. It's like there are all these rules about how you're supposed to be. There's only one path and that's the one you have to follow – if you step off, then that's it, anyone can have a go at you. No one says it, they just know. So, what am I supposed to do about that?"

Atif looks around. For a while, I don't think he's going to say anything else. I shiver and hug myself. It's cooling down and I haven't got a hoodie or anything. Atif's only in short sleeves, he must be cold too but he doesn't seem to mind. Perhaps we should go home. If I can face it.

I'm about to get up, when Atif says, "Do you go running round here then?" He indicates the footpaths leading over the hill behind us.

"Yeah." I pause, remembering. "Actually, a couple of

times when I was younger I'd sneak out without telling Mum or Dad to run up here. Not proper running, just messing about. But it was good, it made me feel free, it was better than anything else. It's how I got started."

Atif nods like he understands.

"But what about the fell running? How did you get into that? I'd never even heard of it until Jo told me about it, I'm afraid."

"Most people haven't. I mean, it's not like you've got any fells in London, is it? I saw this programme about it on TV, when I was in Year Five, and it looked amazing. By the finish, the runners were absolutely *coated* in mud. I already knew I loved running, and this looked far more exciting than just running by myself. I pestered Mum and Dad for weeks about it, googled it, found a local junior club and kept telling them to look at the links. I even got Auntie Jo to nag them about it for me – I mean, she was excited to have another runner in the family. The twins were still really little at the time, so Mum and Dad were a bit distracted, but then they took me along one week, and that was it."

"How hard's the training?"

"Brutal, especially in the winter. It's fun though, it makes me feel...good." What a weak way of putting it. Pathetic. I try to find better words. I want Atif to really get it. "Like, you know it's going to be tough, there's going to be mud and hills and really difficult bits, but you just have to get through them. Even when you think, nah, that's too much. People think it's just about being fit, but it's not, you have to have tactics too – you have to pace yourself, work out your own route and stick to it, stay focused." I can feel myself getting a bit carried away. This is probably the most I've ever said to Atif.

"So, it sounds like you *do* know what to do about school then."

"What?"

"At the risk of sounding cheesy, you're worried about facing tough stuff at school, if people think you're gay or just different, aren't you?" I nod, unsure where this is going. "Maybe stuff that feels harder than running up hills in the mud or whatever. You'll wonder if maybe you're getting it wrong, if you should give up or just follow the same way as everyone else because it's easier. But you know what to do about that. Stick at it. Because it's your path, it's the route you've chosen, the right one for you."

"Yeah," I say, trying to lighten the mood a bit. "Really cheesy." But something about what he's saying makes sense.

"One more thing, while I'm on a roll. When you're running, are you focused behind you or ahead? At the start or the finish?"

"Er...ahead, of course."

"Aidan, you don't have to listen to me. I'm not your mum or dad, I can't tell you what to do, you made it pretty clear earlier on that's what you think." I look at my shoes. Now I wish I hadn't said all those things. "But, one thing – stop running away, okay? Whether it's from things changing or from people who just want to help you and be your friends, but most of all, from yourself. Instead, put all your heart and your soul and your energy into running *towards* the person you want to be, and don't look back." He coughs, a bit embarrassed. "Well, anyway..."

I'm trying to find the right words to say thank you, when Atif's phone rings. So loud it makes us both jump.

He snatches it up from beside him. "Yes...yes...okay... Coming right now."

"Okay to go home?" he asks. I think his voice is shaking a bit, but it could be from the cold. "Justin and I need to get to the hospital now. Kelly and Jack are at your house."

"So, the baby's really coming? Now?"

"Well, it could still take hours, but yes, this is it."

"Do you want to run back?" I ask. "It's all downhill."

"Let's just walk fast," says Atif. "I think that run up here earlier was enough for me."

We stride back down the hill. The clouds have got darker and rain is starting to fall.

I try out the words several times in my head, before I spit them out.

"I'm sorry," I say finally. "I've been an idiot. I shouldn't have said those things, I didn't mean them. I don't think anything's your fault, not really. I shouldn't have run off like that. It's been..." I look for the right word, and can't find it, so just keep going. "It's been all right you being here these last few days. Honest."

"Thanks, it's a hard time for all of us," says Atif. "It's all new to us – remembering who eats what and when bedtime is and what you need for school. I'm not sure we've done a very good job looking after any of you—"

"No," I interrupt. "You have. The girls love you. They really do. You're going to be great dads."

"I hope so." Atif's picked up the pace, so that we are almost jogging down the road now. "I've been trying to reassure Justin. I said to him, it's not like they start out as teenagers. We've got thirteen years to get ready for that—"

"Why's he so worried?"

"His relationship with his own dad wasn't great. I never knew him – he died before Justin and I got together. It just wasn't a happy home by the sound of it. Too much shouting, not enough love. Justin still gets anxious about lots of things. You've probably noticed that he worries too much about whether people like him or not. But, most of all, he always says that he doesn't want to be like his dad. So, tonight, when he lost his temper with you, I think that scared him. He thought that he was turning into his dad after all."

I feel a sudden unexpected surge of gratitude towards Dad. However loud and embarrassing he is, you could never say that our home wasn't happy, or that there wasn't enough love. Never.

I glance at my watch. We've not even been away an hour, though it feels like much longer. Long enough for something to change inside me. Now, it's not just that I'm thankful for the family I've got. For the first time, I feel lucky that Justin and Atif – and their new baby – are part of our family too.

Chapter Eighteen

"Do we have to watch the whole thing?" yawns Jack. "Don't they have highlights or something? All we need is to check out some of the costumes and to see that exciting bit when the winner breaks through the tape at the end."

"We're watching it *all*," I tell him. "We don't want to miss seeing Auntie Jo. Here, do you want some toast?"

"Yeah, go on, put in a couple of slices for me. There's no way you'll see her on TV. There's forty thousand runners and she's not even dressing up – despite me giving her all my best suggestions."

"Will you stop going on about dressing up? It's not about the costumes, it's about the running."

"Yeah, yeah." He reaches up to get a jar of peanut butter out of the cupboard. Jack's spent so much time in our house that he knows exactly where to find everything. "Still though, if *I* was doing it, *I'd* dress up."

"You'd never do it though, would you? It's a marathon. 26.2 miles. You won't even run for the bus."

"Aidan Conor Taylor, stop puncturing my dreams with such petty details!" he answers back.

The house is quiet. Bells is still in her room, probably asleep, and Jack's mum has taken Chloe, the twins and Toto to the Field to run around.

Last night was a different story. Everyone dashing about, trying to sort stuff out. Bells, Jack and I helped his mum settle the younger ones in bed, but they were too hyped up to go to sleep for ages. They only stopped talking when we promised we'd tell them as soon as the baby came, even if it was in the middle of the night.

By that time, I was done in too. Jack's mum slept on the sofa. Jack slept in a sleeping bag on my bedroom floor. We didn't talk about school or Mum or Justin and Atif at all. Instead, it was like sleepovers when we were little, with Jack doing silly voices and making terrible jokes, and me trying not to laugh because I knew, once I'd started, I'd be unable to stop. It felt good to mess around. Especially after the conversation with Atif yesterday – that was heavy. I'm still working out what to do with what he said.

"We might as well watch it all," I say. "What else are we

going to do while we're waiting for something to happen?"

"What did your dad say in his last message?"

I shrug. "Not much. Mum's okay. No baby yet."

"And what about you? Are you okay?"

"Course I'm okay."

The toast pops. I smother both mine and Jack's in peanut butter, and we take our plates through to the living room, ready for breakfast in front of the TV.

"It's just that I really thought you'd done a runner yesterday. I didn't know what was going on when Atif came banging on our door. He looked well shaken up."

"I know, I feel rubbish about it. Disappearing like that. Giving everyone all that extra stress."

Jack smiles. "Come on, don't beat yourself up about it. I quite enjoyed the drama to be honest." I know he's just saying that to try to make me feel better. It's almost working.

"I was a bit disappointed when Atif said he didn't need me to come, that he'd go and look for you by himself," he continues. "It was okay to tell him where I thought you'd be, wasn't it?"

"Yeah, no worries," I say. "You got it right first guess. I'm so boring and predictable, I couldn't even think of anywhere decent to run away to."

"It's not that you're predictable, it's just that *I* know you too well." He puts on a voice like he's a scheming villain in a James Bond film. "You have no secrets from me, Agent Taylor." Then he goes red, his normal voice kicks in again and he stumbles over his words. "Oh, I'm sorry, I didn't mean to make it sound like that, like you always *have* to tell me everything. I mean, you don't, it's..."

"Okay, Jack, I get it, thanks."

We both stare at the screen, chewing our toast and watching wave upon wave of runners jog across the start line. There's a man dressed as a loo roll who keeps waving at the camera. When Jack opens his mouth, I'm sure he's about to point this out as a good example of an eye-catching costume, but instead he says, "You and Atif were up there for ages yesterday. When Mum and I got round here, Justin was jumping all over the place, really nervous. How did Atif persuade you to come back home?"

I swallow my mouthful too quickly, which makes me cough. I always have that problem with eating peanut butter. It goes all claggy in the back of my throat. Jack thumps me hard on the back until I wave my hands in the air to get him to stop.

"It wasn't like that," I say when I finally have my breath back. Then, I stop, trying to think about what it *was* like, and how to explain that to Jack. "Actually, Atif's okay. They both are really."

Jack raises his eyebrows. "Okaaaaay?" he says questioningly.

"And...I did what you said, ages ago. I talked to him. We talked about, well..." I pause, distracted by the progress of the human loo roll on the screen in front of me. I just hope it doesn't rain today – he looks very absorbent. "Okay, we talked about...being gay."

"And?" says Jack.

"And...you were right, he really listened. I wasn't joking before about being gay. I don't know why I even said I was. It was stupid. So, I don't know, but I think, maybe I am, yes."

This is awful. It is so embarrassing that I can't believe that I'm still sitting here and not curled up in a ball of shame in the corner. I so should have done this by text, like last time, not face to face. I can't look at Jack. He doesn't say anything. Maybe he's angry about how I messed him about before.

When I finally pluck up the courage to look up, he's grinning.

"So, I was right, was I? You did what I said?" he says, waving his toast a little too close to my face in his excitement. "I gave you my wise advice about talking to Atif or Justin and you followed it, even if it took you for ever, that *is* what happened?"

"Yes, okay, I said you were right, didn't I? No need to go on about it."

"Hah." He leans back on the sofa, satisfied. "So, you *are* gay? Cool. Who else have you come out to?"

"No one," I say in horror.

"So, I'm the first, apart from Atif?" he asks.

I nod.

"Ah, thanks, mate." He gives me a nudge. "I'm honoured. So, who are you going to tell next?"

"For god's sake, Jack, give us a break. Isn't this enough?"

"Yeah, all right." He reluctantly turns his attention back to the TV. "Are they *still* going?"

"It's only been ten minutes," I say.

"*... Our team of celebrity reporters are out and about today, finding out about as many as possible of the inspirational causes motivating these amazing runners...*" enthuses the commentator's voice from the TV. Someone I don't recognize but who must be a celebrity reporter starts interviewing the loo roll as she trots alongside him.

I'm not really watching, instead I'm running over the last few minutes in my mind. I breathe out slowly. I told Atif. I told Jack. I told them. And nothing dreadful happened. A warm feeling spreads through me. Almost like when you get into a hot bath, and you feel your muscles start relaxing, even if you hadn't realized how tense they were. I'm smiling and I can't stop.

"You know what?" says Jack out of nowhere. "You could have kids one day too. Like Atif and Justin."

"Shut up," I say, though I'm still grinning.

But there's something else. Something that's still not quite right. Something that makes me stop smiling.

"Jack?" I say tentatively.

"Uh huh?" he asks.

"All that stuff, with Ethan and Sam and the others, and with Mr Evans. Did it just stop, or...?"

There's such a long silence that I wonder if he's heard me.

"No," sighs Jack finally. "It didn't stop, but I just kind of tune it out now, you know, like irritating background noise. I can't help other people being ignorant, can I? It's not so bad if I just ignore it. Honest. After that stuff with my uniform, Mum wanted to go into school, but I begged her not to. After that, I've just pretended that it's okay."

"And *is* it okay?"

"It's okay enough. There's times when I want to say or do something, but I stop myself, it feels safer like that. I know I'm still me, underneath. I can still act and dress up and mess around, and even paint my nails..." He flashes his fingers briefly at me. "…just not all the time. Anyway, it's not long till the end of the year, then hopefully I'll get a different PE teacher, and I won't have to have anything to do with Mr Evans ever again. I can't wait."

"But that's not fair," I say. "You shouldn't have to change who you are just because other people are idiots. And Mr Evans, he shouldn't be able to get away with having a go at you, just because he's a teacher."

"I know," says Jack. "But he does."

Half an hour later, the others aren't back yet, and Jack and I still haven't moved from the sofa. I check my phone every minute, but there's nothing from the hospital.

"No news is good news, right?" Jack says, when he sees me looking for the thousandth time.

"What?"

"It's a saying: no news is good news. My mum says it all the time."

I think about this. It makes no sense. "No offence to your mum, but it's a stupid saying. If there's no news, how can you know if it's good or bad?"

"Yeah," says Jack. "I guess so."

I look at the dirty plates on the floor. I can't leave them there. I don't want Mum and Dad to come back and think that I didn't know how to look after myself. So I gather up mine and Jack's and start to take them through to the kitchen. Then I spot someone familiar out of the corner of my eye. It takes me a moment to recognize her because she's in costume.

"Look, Jack, it's her, it's Auntie Jo, on the TV. Pause it, pause it. My hands are full."

"Hang on, where's the remote?" Jack uncurls himself from the saggy sofa and starts frantically rummaging under the cushions. "I can't find it!"

"Hello," calls Jack's mum loudly from the hallway, as the door bangs shut. "Are you up yet? It's lovely out."

"Yeah, we're up. But, shush, it's Auntie Jo, on TV. Come in, quick!"

"Ah, that's *it*!" says Jack as he freezes the image of Auntie Jo on the screen. Tower Bridge looms behind her. "Shall I go back?"

Chloe, Evie and Daisy pile into the living room. Their faces are all red from running around outside and they've still got their shoes on.

"What's the noise about?" says Bells, sticking her head round the door. Then she looks at the screen. "No way. It's her. Go on, play it."

"I thought she said she wasn't wearing a costume," protests Jack.

"She wasn't," I say, but it's definitely Auntie Jo, and she's definitely dressed as a doctor, in green surgical scrubs, with a stethoscope round her neck and her hair held back under one of those medical caps.

Jack shushes us all down and then presses play. The interviewer asks Auntie Jo who she's raising money for and what motivated her to run. I watch him closely as he leans in to ask the questions.

"For my local maternity unit," she says. She looks very comfortable, barely short of breath. All that training, I guess. "I've not used it myself, but all five of my nieces and nephews were born there."

"That's us!" says Evie excitedly. "She's talking about us. On TV. Are we famous?"

"Shush," says Bells fiercely.

"In fact, my sister's in there right now," continues Auntie Jo.

"What's your sister's name?" asks the interviewer.

Auntie Jo turns her back to the interviewer, still jogging along. On her back is a handwritten sign: "*Running for Laura*".

"That's Mummy's name," says Daisy, pointing at the screen.

"Well, we hope all goes well for Laura. And for you – good luck, I won't hold you up any more." Auntie Jo waves at the camera and we watch her run off, before it cuts to a different interviewer shoving his mike in front of a woman who looks like she must be in her 80s. Her T-shirt is printed with the slogan: "*30th marathon and counting*".

"Is Auntie Jo famous?" asks Evie. No one shushes her this time, instead we're all talking at once.

"Yeah, definitely," Bells tells her. "I'm messaging her right now to say we saw her on TV."

"Don't be stupid," I say. "She's not going to be checking her phone now, she's still got, like, fourteen miles to go."

"Who was that bloke interviewing her?" asks Jack. "He looked familiar."

"Oh yes," says his mum. "He did, it's on the tip of my tongue. He used to be on Blue Peter when you were younger."

"Yeah, but he reminds me of someone else too. This is so annoying. Who is it?"

I shrug.

"I know," says Jack suddenly, pointing up in the air in triumph. "It's Lily's brother, isn't it? It's Will. Don't you think, Aidan, Bells? That's who he reminds me of, they've got the same smile."

"Dunno," I say, reaching down to pick up the plates again so that he can't see my face. "Hadn't really noticed." I take the dishes through to the kitchen. Until just now, I've barely thought about Will for days, there's been so much else filling my head. Lily telling me about Jen and Will feels like a lifetime ago.

"Oh my god!" shouts Jack's mum suddenly, so loud that I can hear her in the kitchen. I slam the plates down on the side and dash back through. She and Bells are both holding their phones. I look from one face to the other. They both look like they're crying. What has happened? Is it Mum? Has something gone wrong?

But they're smiling too.

"What *is* it?" But before either of them can reply, I snatch up my phone from the side of the sofa. Typical, the first time I take my eyes off it all morning, and that's when a new message arrives. I guess it's the same one that Jack's mum and Bells have just got. My hands have gone all sweaty. It takes me three goes to get the passcode right. It's from Dad.

"It's fine," says Jack's mum, in between sniffs. "Sorry, it's just that, Justin and Atif have got a little boy. He's small, only five pounds, one ounce, the lads are with him now. Your dad says the staff think he'll need a bit of extra care, but he's going to be fine. Oh, what a relief, come here everyone…" She squashes all of us into a giant hug, with arms and legs sticking out in all directions. It's hard to read the rest of the message on my phone with Chloe's elbows jabbing into my side and Evie jumping up and down on my toes with excitement.

My first thought is, wow, at last, there's finally another boy in the family, I've finally got a brother. Except I haven't. This baby's not really my brother at all.

"What about Mum?" I ask.

"She's absolutely fine, that's what your dad says."

"Can we go and see her?" asks Bells.

"Soon, but not right now. She probably just needs to sleep. She'll be exhausted. Although, after I'd had you, Jack, I was wide awake and all I wanted to do was eat. I kept asking the midwife if I was allowed a bacon sandwich. Your dad'll be on his way home soon. He'll need to crash out, but I bet he's dying to see you all."

I slump down onto the sofa. Suddenly shattered, like I've been running for miles myself, instead of just watching other people doing it on TV. Weirdly happy too, like I might burst out laughing any moment. I think everyone else feels the same. No one says anything. We all just look at each other with these big daft grins on our faces. Thank goodness. This is the news we've all been waiting for. Now we can start to relax. I glance at the screen, the runners are still going. They've not reached the finish yet, but they're getting closer, they're on their way.

Chapter Nineteen

"God, what a time to do it," moans India as we wait outside Ms Ashby's office on Monday morning. "I couldn't even work out what to have for breakfast this morning – now I've got to decide what I'm studying for the next two years."

I don't know India that well, but I like her. She makes people laugh not by being mean about other people, but because of the sideways way she sees the world. Jack knows her better than I do, from the school plays, but India and I are next to each other in the register – Aidan Taylor, India Thorn – so we often end up in the same groups.

"Haven't you already decided?" I ask. "I thought this was the last bit, where it all got finally signed off."

"I decided what I *didn't* want to do. That was easy," she

sighs. "But apparently *just* doing Drama and Textiles for GCSE is not considered a balanced education."

I laugh. "Those would both be top of my list *not* to pick."

"I don't get why Ms Ashby wants to see all of us, one by one. We've already filled in the forms."

"I guess she just wants to check. In case we've got any last-minute changes or something."

She gives an exaggerated yawn, like all this talk of GCSE options is boring her rigid. "How was your weekend, Aidan? Anything exciting happen?"

I wonder how she'd react if I say: *nothing much – except I ran away from home, my mum had a baby, I came out to my best friend and my aunt was on TV.*

"What you smiling about?" she asks. "Was it *that* good?"

"Nah, quiet really, you know, family stuff."

"Uh huh," she says, losing interest in my weekend. "Well, you know it was Olivia's party on Saturday, oh my god…" And she launches into a long description of who was there and what happened and what everyone was saying about it this morning. She's still going when Pav Singh walks out of the office and shuts the door behind him.

"You can go in now," he says to me.

"Take ages," hisses India. "Like, really spin it out, then I might get to miss all of Spanish."

That's so not going to happen. I know what GCSEs I want to do. I should be in and out within a minute. My head's not in the right place for a long conversation anyway, it's still full of everything that happened this weekend.

Ms Ashby looks up at me with a vague expression on her face, then shuffles some papers in front of her. She's been my form teacher all year but I still don't think she's entirely sure who I am – not one of the troublemakers, not one of the people who volunteers for things, just quietly getting on with my own stuff.

"So, Aidan?" she says questioningly, peering at me through her glasses.

"Yes, Miss."

"This all looks fairly straightforward. French, Geography, PE as your options, beyond the ones you have to take, of course. All your teachers for those subjects are very happy to have you in their GCSE classes. Is there anything you want to ask about the process?"

"No, Miss." I'm going to be out of here in no time. India's going to be so unimpressed.

"And, generally?" she says, leaning back in her chair, pressing her fingers together. "How are things going? All the attention's on Years Ten and Eleven, you know, the GCSE years, but Year Nine can be a tough one too. Making choices, moving up the school, some people find it an uphill struggle at times."

"Not me, I'm fine," I say, then add quickly, "thank you." She waits for just a couple of beats before saying anything. I shift in my seat.

"Okay then, give India a shout to come in."

Ms Ashby turns her attention back to her papers. I guess she has a lot of Year Nines to get through today. I'm almost at the door when her words hit me: an uphill struggle. They make me think of Atif, what he said about taking the right path, even if it's the difficult one.

I know what I should do. But I don't want to. I just want to get out of here and get on with my day. My heart starts pounding and my feet are ready to run.

But then, perhaps it's meant to be. It's not like I went looking for someone to tell. I'm here anyway. Anyone would just think I'm talking about GCSE options. Like they'd care.

"Miss…?" I say. She looks up again. "There is this one thing."

"Go on."

"It's, well, it's about Mr Evans."

"I didn't think he was your PE teacher," says Ms Ashby,

flicking through the papers. "It's Ms Pattison who's signed off your GCSE choice, isn't it?"

"Yes…but this isn't about GCSEs."

I pause, not sure what to say next. What if she doesn't believe me?

"Come on then, stop hovering," Ms Ashby says finally. "Sit down and tell me what it *is* about."

And, the best I can, with a lot of "um"s and false starts, I tell her about Jack, what's been happening to him in PE and the sorts of things that Mr Evans has been saying. As soon as she realizes what I'm talking about she stops looking vague. She leans forward, taking in every word, asking questions and noting down what I say. She seems interested but not necessarily surprised. I don't say too much about what happened after school, just try to focus on Mr Evans. I certainly don't tell Ms Ashby any names, even though she tries to push me to.

When I finish talking and she finishes firing questions at me, she takes off her glasses and rubs her eyes.

"Okay, Aidan, thank you for telling me. That was very helpful. Now, are you okay to leave this with me? I will be following it up." I can tell by her voice that she means it.

I nod, but there's one thing that I'm still worried about. "You won't tell Jack, will you, or Mr Evans, that it was me that told you?" I say anxiously.

"Not if you don't want me to."

"Thanks, Miss."

When I get out of the office, India gives me a big thumbs up.

"That was ace, you were in there for ages. Dunno what you were saying, but well done."

I trudge slowly back to the classroom. I had tried to persuade Dad to let me off school today, but no, he said that we all had to go in. It was too late to see Mum yesterday, so we're not going till after school today. I don't think anything will seem quite real until I see her. I just need to get through the rest of the day's lessons first.

After school, Bells and I get the bus straight to the hospital, instead of going home first. Dad's decided it would be too tiring for Mum if everyone goes in at once, so we're going in two batches. I'm sure everyone else in there will be pleased about that too – they don't need the whole of Team Taylor descending at once. Dad's taking Chloe, Evie and Daisy in first as they finish school earlier. Then Bells and I are meeting Auntie Jo outside and the three of us will go in together.

Auntie Jo's easy to spot, standing at the entrance to the maternity ward, holding a massive sparkly balloon with "Congratulations" across it. She waves us over and then envelops us both in a huge hug.

"I'm *so* sorry," she says. "I should have been here this weekend, what with all this going on. What kind of aunt am I? Are you both okay?"

"Yeah, fine," says Bells breezily. "We saw you on TV. You *were* wearing a costume after all."

"I know," says Auntie Jo, grimacing. "My friends persuaded me in the end, they bought all the bits I needed. But make sure you tell Jack that it was all down to him, it was his idea, okay?"

"How are you?" I ask. "Are you aching? You must be so sore."

"I thought I would be, but I'm not too bad actually. I'm sure having a baby is harder than running a marathon anyway so I can't complain. Here, I've got something to show you. Hold this balloon a sec." She passes the balloon to me and then reaches her hand inside her jumper and pulls out her medal. It's on a red ribbon and it's much bigger and heavier than I thought it would be. "I mean, it's not as flash as the Under-14s cup's going to be, but…" She grins at me.

"Yeah, well, season's not over yet," I say, trying to play it down just in case. Trying to win the cup isn't the reason I go running, but I can't help imagining how great it would be if I did.

"I've got some other bits in my bag," she says. "They

give you all this free stuff if you take part, it's great. I reckon I've got something for everyone, even if it's just a few leaflets for the twins. They could cut them up for craft or something. It's nothing much, but seeing as you couldn't be there after all, I thought you'd like a little part of the day. Here, Bells, this is some kind of relaxing shower gel, I think." She hands Bells a small bottle. "And, Aidan, these are cool, they were giving these away too, I thought you could have them on your trainers." She hands me a pair of bright rainbow-coloured laces.

"Er, thanks," I say. They're quite in-your-face. Although after a few minutes on a run, they'd be so covered in mud that no one would know what colours they'd started out anyway.

"Come on, we better go in and see your mum. She'll be made up to see you both."

We have to tell the nurse behind the desk our names and how we're related to Mum before she'll let us through. I'm starting to feel nervous. Despite all the recent visits, I'm still not the biggest fan of hospitals.

I wish Mum could come home right now and everything could start to go back to normal again. Except I don't know if it can, or even if I really want it to. Not after everything that's happened, everything that's changed.

Mum's in a different ward from before – one where you

can hear the sound of babies crying as you walk down the corridor – but apart from that, it's weird, because nothing seems very different from when we last came, before Mum had the baby. She's still in bed, looking almost as big as before and only slightly more tired. Her stack of magazines and snacks has grown and there are more hand-drawn pictures from Chloe and the twins by the side of the bed.

"Laura!" exclaims Auntie Jo as soon as she spots Mum.

"Look at that balloon," says Mum. "It's enormous – I can hardly see Aidan behind it." I feel a bit daft standing there holding it, but I can't work out where to put it.

I'm not really sure what to say to Mum first. Should I ask about the baby or not?

"I know, I got carried away," says Auntie Jo. "I wasn't sure you'd be allowed flowers, and then it took ages to find a balloon that wasn't pink or blue. Just wait though, I've got you something even better." She produces three packets of salt-and-vinegar crisps from her bag and waves them in front of Mum. "Ta da."

"Oh," says Mum. "Thanks, love, but I've gone off them now. I think they'd even turn my stomach a bit. Sorry."

"I'll have a packet," I say quickly.

"Me too," chips in Bells.

"Well, that leaves one for me then," says Auntie Jo.

And then we perch on chairs next to Mum's bed and

chat and eat crisps and she asks us about school, and it's not weird and awkward any more. It's just like always, like we're back home from school and her child-minding kids have been picked up and Auntie Jo's popped in after work and it's any normal day.

"Jo," says Mum after we've chatted for a bit. "I'm parched. Do you reckon you could fill up this bottle of water for me? There's a little kitchen area just down the corridor."

"Sure," says Auntie Jo. "Fancy coming with me, Bells? We can have a bit of a snoop around."

"Scoot up a bit closer," Mum says to me when they've gone. I move further up the bed. "It's so good to see you. I feel like I've been in here for ever. I can't wait to get home, be a proper family again. Fingers crossed they check me out tomorrow." She pauses. "Aidan, listen, is there anything else you want to know about the baby? You can ask anything, you know."

From not knowing what to say earlier, now my mind is suddenly full of questions. I know Mum would answer them all. In fact, she probably engineered this chance to be alone with me, just so I could ask. But *how* do I ask them? Where do I start?

"Did you see him?" I ask. "What's he like?"

"Yes, I did," says Mum gently. "Enough to say hello,

then the staff checked him over and Justin and Atif got to have a cuddle with him. Such a tiny scrap of a thing, a bit like Evie and Daisy were. Not like you, you were much bigger when you were born. A right little bruiser. You know there's some problems with his liver, your dad would have said, so he needs to have this special light box treatment for a few days. There's a room for him and Justin and Atif to stay where the nurses can keep an eye on them, just down the hall. I can go and see him whenever I want, but I thought no, give his dads their time. I'll go later on though. You could try and see him before you leave today. It's important. But for now, do you want to see a photo?"

I nod. A photo's enough for me right now. Mum pulls out her phone and shows me a picture of a tiny baby in a plastic box. Only his head's visible, the rest of his body is covered with blue material. That must be the light box. I squint at the picture for a bit, looking for clues. But you can't tell whether or not he looks like any of us – he just looks like a baby, any baby. You couldn't even tell whether it's a boy or a girl, unless you knew already.

I swipe back to the photo before. One of the midwives must have taken it just after the birth. The baby's wrapped in a blanket, Justin holding him tightly and Atif looking down at the bundle in his arms. They both have the same look on their faces. The three of them look like they belong together. They look like a family.

"What was it like to...?" I hesitate.

"What?" asks Mum.

"...to give him away?" I finish.

She sighs. "At first, I was just so tired, and so relieved that I was okay and the baby was okay despite all that drama, and that I'd done what I set out to do, that I didn't really think about it. This was always going to happen, you know that, this was never my baby, even though he's always going to be part of our lives. Honestly, it didn't feel like I was giving him away. It felt like I was giving him back. I'm so proud and happy for Justin and Atif. It's pretty amazing to think that we helped them create their little family."

"So, was it different to how it was with us?" I ask. "Like, could you have imagined being able to give away Bells or Chloe or the twins or...me?" At first, I'm just curious. But by the time I've finished asking the question, I realize that I really need to know. Because if Mum can give away this baby so easily, then what does that mean about how she feels about the rest of us?

"Never," says Mum straight away, almost before I've finished speaking. "Never, never, never, okay?"

"Yeah, okay." I'm surprised by how fierce she is.

"And it's still the same, even now you're all growing up. There's nothing any of you could do or be or become that would mean that I could ever imagine not being proud to be your mum." She's sitting forward in bed now and I think there might even be tears in her eyes. I'm worried I might get in trouble with the nurses for overexciting her or something.

"All right, Mum, calm down."

"Well, it's important you know that." She squeezes my hand, still sounding a bit choked up.

I wasn't planning to, not today, but this would be the ideal moment to tell her I'm gay. It would be so easy, so right. The words are waiting. I open my mouth, ready.

"Here we go," says Auntie Jo, returning to the ward. "Sorry we took so long. We bumped into Justin in the corridor, and he took us into their room to see the baby. Oh, Laura, he's beautiful. And they looked so happy, didn't they, Bells?"

I jump to my feet and start moving things around on the little table next to the bed to make room for the bottle of water. I'm a bit shaky, all that emotion from Mum and the way I'd psyched myself up to talk to her, and I knock the pile of magazines to the floor.

The moment for telling her's gone. I bend down to pick up the magazines, secretly relieved that Bells and

Auntie Jo came back when they did. I know now that whenever I tell Mum it will be fine. It could be now or next week or not for years, that doesn't matter. Or it could be one of those things that doesn't need any big drama or announcement. Come to think of it, I bet Mum already knows. It's only me that's taken this long to work it out. If I can be okay with it, then I reckon everyone else can be too. Or if they're not, that's not my problem. I smile to myself. Jack would be proud of me, I think.

JULY

Chapter Twenty

I'm finishing off a gigantic bowl of Weetabix, and getting ready to start on some toast, when the doorbell rings. It can't be Auntie Jo already, there's still at least half an hour before we have to leave. I haven't even checked through all my kit yet.

It's the last race of the season today. Straight afterwards, they'll tot up the points and give out the cups for the different ages and a few special awards for newcomers and improvers too. It's a bit of an occasion – everyone gathers round and claps for the winners and tells stories of the best moments of the year.

If I do well today – even better if I win – then that Under-14s cup is mine. The cup goes to the runner with the five fastest times across the season and I've raced really well the whole time. Despite everything else going on. Or maybe because of it. Running's been a place to escape, where I can push myself to my limits and push everything else out of my mind. I've poured all my emotions – anger, worry, fear, the lot – into running better, faster, harder.

Today, I just need to keep calm. Stay focused.

Except it's not easy to stay focused with Bells and Lily chatting away at top volume over breakfast. Lily slept over here last night and I bet they stayed up all night talking too. I definitely heard Dad get up and shush them at least twice.

There's voices in the hallway. Then Jack comes into the kitchen and sits down next to me.

"All right? Your mum said you were having breakfast." He sounds really upbeat today. Even more than usual. I wonder what's up.

"Have a drink then." I push the orange juice towards him and he goes and gets himself a glass out of the cupboard.

"Ready for the race? You were really good last time."

"Dunno." I don't want to tempt my good luck to disappear by being overconfident. "This one's harder though. I don't really know the course."

"You'll be fine," says Jack in his usual confident way, then he puffs out his chest, claps me on the shoulder and puts on a deep voice, "Of course you will, you're Team Taylor!"

Bells and Lily laugh. Jack has captured Dad's body language perfectly.

"Ha, ha," I say. "Thanks, Dad."

I stand up, put my bowl in the dishwasher, then prop my foot up on the kitchen chair to tie my shoes.

"I like your laces," says Lily.

"Auntie Jo got them at the marathon," I tell her. "They were giving them away. I think they're too bright, but I guess she'll want to see me wear them today."

"They're cool," continues Lily. "Are the rainbows for the NHS or something?"

"No," says Jack, leaning over to look. It feels weird to have everyone in the room staring at my feet. "I've seen them before on TV. It's part of this LGBTQ equality thing."

I was hoping no one would ask about the laces, or that they'd be totally covered in mud before anyone noticed. Since talking with Atif, I've been looking up gay athletes online. He was right, there's loads of them, all kinds of sports, and lots were wearing these laces. I'm not sure Auntie Jo knows any of that, I reckon she just liked the colours.

"What do *you* know about sport?" I ask Jack.

"Very little," he says. "But I *do* know a lot about style!"

"So, it's a gay thing?" says Lily, confused. "But Aidan you're not..."

Then there's silence. Silence that seems to go on and on and on. I can't think of the right words to say, so I don't say anything. Even Jack keeps quiet.

Lily goes bright red. Bells's mouth falls open.

"You didn't tell me!" says Bells, her voice higher than usual.

"I don't have to tell you everything," I say.

"So, are you and Jack, like, a thing?" she asks, looking from one of us to the other and back again.

"No!" we both say in unison.

"You know what?" says Jack. "I'm seriously thinking of getting a T-shirt specially made. It would say something like, '*I'm not gay, but my best mate is*' and there'd be an arrow underneath pointing to him. Just to help clear things up, you know."

"So, you *are* gay?" Bells says to me.

"No need to tell the whole street!"

"Bells," says Lily in an urgent whisper, pulling at my sister's arm. "Can we go upstairs?"

"What?" says Bells, and then she looks at Lily's face. "All right then." She shoots me a look as she shuts the door. "Tell me everything later, Aidan. I mean it."

"Awkward," says Jack, wincing.

"Oh god," I say, head in my hands. "That so wasn't meant to happen. I've really upset Lily now. Should I go and say something to her?"

I don't want to, but maybe I should.

"Like what?" says Jack. "She'll get over it. You're not like the only lad in the world, are you? It's better like this, she can think you don't fancy her cos you're gay, not just that you don't fancy her full stop."

"I guess so." I'm not convinced that's how Lily will see it, not today anyway.

Something else strikes me. "Do you reckon Bells is going to tell *everyone* now?"

"Probably, but that's for the best, right? Then *you* don't have to. It's not a big deal anyway. It's cool."

"Wow," I say. "You really are Mr Every-Cloud-Has-A-Silver-Lining today, what's up?"

"Well," says Jack, settling into full storytelling mode. "This really weird thing happened on Friday at school. You'll never believe it."

"Yeah? Try me."

"Mr Evans stopped me in the corridor and asked if he could have a word. So, I got in a right panic because I was so sure he was going to have a go."

"But he didn't?"

"No, that's the weird bit. He said sorry."

"He said what?"

Jack's right, I don't believe it.

"I know. I thought I wasn't hearing him right or something. But he did, he said sorry for singling me out in front of the class, and he said that he realized he'd made some 'unwise comments that he now regretted'." Jack pauses. "I mean, they were more than 'unwise', but anyway. And he said that, even though he won't be teaching me in Year Ten – thank god – he hoped we could start afresh. Neither of us *said* 'thank god' but I reckon we were both thinking it. He even said if I got any trouble from anyone else in the class that I should come straight to him."

"Wow," I say. "Where did that come from?"

"Dunno." Jack shrugs. "Didn't you say you saw him at the hospital back when you were visiting your mum? Maybe having a new baby has made him all soft."

"Maybe," I say, but I don't think that's the real reason. I think my talk with Ms Ashby might have had something to do with it. It was weeks ago now. I wondered whether she was ever going to do anything, but it looks like she did after all.

"I don't know why," says Jack, reaching over to nick a bit of toast off my plate. "But if this means that he's off my case now, I don't care why."

Jack takes a large bite and settles back in his chair.

"Why are you here anyway?" I ask. "You know I've got a race this morning, I'm going in a few minutes. Did you just come to steal my breakfast?"

"Not just that, although I might have another slice of toast as I'm here. No, Mum sent me over. She lent your mum this foot spa, ages ago, and now she wants it again, 'cept your mum says she already gave it back. It's okay, my mum probably got confused and lent it to someone else."

"Oh," I say. "Actually, no, she didn't get confused, it's my fault. Come upstairs."

"What?" asks Jack, but he follows me anyway.

I drag the box out from under the bed. It's heavy and hard to get a decent hold on.

"Why have you been hiding my mum's foot spa under your bed, Ade?" asks Jack, genuinely confused. "What other secrets have you got under there? Buried treasure? Dead bodies? I mean, now's the time to tell me if there's anything else you want to get off your chest."

"Don't be stupid," I say. I spot a crumpled envelope on the floor and quickly stuff it in my pocket. Moving the box must have dislodged it from its hiding place. It's the list I made of reasons for and against me being gay. "It's complicated. I didn't mean to keep it, it's just… Oh never mind, here, take it. Your mum will be pleased."

"Thanks," says Jack, as I awkwardly hand the box over to him, glad to get rid of it at last. I grip the envelope in my pocket, scrunching it into a ball in my fist. It feels like so long ago that I sat down and wrote that list. No one knew then, but now they do, a few people at least. Back then, I thought that it would be the end of the world to come out to anyone. But now, the reasons against – the stuff about not liking rainbows or pink or glitter – seem so ridiculous. As if every LGBTQ person fits the same stereotype or likes the same things.

"Doorbell," says Jack, helpfully.

I'm still in a bit of a dream. When I don't respond, Jack swings his arms round and nudges me with the box. "Wake up, Aidan, time to go. Ready for another fun morning running through the mud? I wish I could join you, but..."

"Ow, shut up!" I say, rubbing my arm. "I'm coming."

Auntie Jo's standing at the door chatting to Mum when I get down the stairs.

"It's great you're able to come with us," says Mum. "After the drama at the last race, I'm determined to make it right through to the end this time, especially as it's Aidan's last one of the season."

"Too right. Anyway, I have to go back to the club and say thank you, after all that money they raised for me."

"And all those cakes they ate!" says Mum. "I'm a bit

worried about leaving the cat though, to be honest. It's the longest we've been out of the house since we got him."

"He'll be okay, you know how independent cats are. How's he settling in?"

"Well, it wasn't easy to find a rescue cat that would be happy with children and a dog, but I think this little fella's starting to feel right at home with us."

Since Justin and Atif left the hospital and the three of them went back to London, the house has felt strange – like something's missing. Even when we're all at home. Even when the three of them come up to visit. Getting a cat was Mum's idea, although everyone's excited about it. Chloe most of all, she's over the moon. Or as Dad likes to say, she's having kittens about it. Ha ha. That's why we all agreed to let her choose the name for him. But, now that she's decided on *Dorothy*, I'm not so sure that was a good idea.

It's weeks since I last raced. So much has happened since then. I've been to training every week, of course, but this is different. I think Auntie Jo can tell I'm feeling nervous, because she leans over and gives my arm a squeeze as I get out of the car.

"Good luck," she says. "You'll smash it. See you afterwards. Okay?"

Two different voices are arguing in my head. One says

that today I have to really push myself, not allow myself to make any mistakes, do my very, very best, only then can I be sure of winning the cup. The other is much calmer, telling me not to worry: whether I win or lose, no one will think any the worse of me. They are both right. I need them both today.

I check I've got all my kit and then jog over to join Charlie, Jon and the others by the start. The younger age groups have already set off on their races. Everyone chats and jokes a bit, but before long, the race begins.

It's drizzling, but still quite warm. The ground's hard and dry, and there's barely any mud today. My rainbow laces stand out pretty strongly, but maybe it's only me that notices.

We start off skirting the edge of a field, go over a stile, and then I have to pick my way down a stony path, slipping every now and again on loose pebbles, but never losing my balance. Just as I force myself up the slope to reach the other side of the valley, the sun comes out from behind a cloud, almost blinding me.

I hold up my arm to shade my eyes and squint, trying to pick out the best route. I try not to think about anyone else, just me, where I need to go next. I'm not even distracted when the sun and rain combine into a rainbow, a double one, hovering in the sky ahead of me. It's just weather. I'm not the sort of person who believes in signs. And yet…this does feel like a good one.

So I push on. My whole body working together to reach the finish. I'm near the front, but I can hear feet pounding and heavy breathing behind me. All I can do is keep going.

At first, I don't realize I've come first. I just keep on running. Charlie and Jon are so close behind me. But before I know it, they're slapping me on the back and congratulating me, so it must be true.

I'll get the cup now, no doubt. But that's not the most important thing. I can see Mum and Dad and Auntie Jo heading towards me, huge smiles on their faces.

For once, I don't care how embarrassing Mum and Dad are bound to be. I can just imagine the crushing hugs, the shouts, the fist bumps. Maybe Mum will even cry. But what matters is that they are on my side and always will be. And I'm on theirs. Team Taylor.

Later, as we gather for the cups to be given out, Auntie Jo makes sure she's standing next to me. "Did you see that rainbow?" she asks. "It was a beauty. You know what they say about rainbows?"

I make a non-committal sort of noise.

"That there's a pot of gold at the end, of course. And there certainly is for me, another couple of people just gave me some money for the marathon. I'm well over the target now, even without Justin's extra help."

"That's brilliant," I say.

"And what about you? You'll be getting your own treasure today. Well, okay, I'm sure that cup isn't real gold, but you know what I mean. I'm really proud of you, Aidan, for everything."

Charlie's dad taps the mike and the sound system whistles with feedback. There's a chorus of moans and everyone puts their hands over their ears.

"Sorry, sorry," he apologizes, before launching into a lengthy account of the ups and downs of this year's season. Someone at the back shouts at him to get on with it and everybody laughs. We're all tired and sweaty but enjoying being outside and together, feeling the warmth of the sun on our backs.

It's all very informal, which suits me, and there are no big speeches when the cups are given out or the volunteers are thanked, just cheering and whistling and big grins.

I freeze for a moment when I hear my name being called, but Auntie Jo pushes me forward and my feet remember how to work again. I dash up to the front, collect the Under-14s cup, and slip back among the crowd as quickly as I can. But this is one time when I don't mind too much that everyone's staring at me. The cup feels good, the weight of the metal, cool and smooth in my warm hands. Something that's mine, that I earned, and will never be passed down to Bells or Chloe or Daisy or Evie.

"These cups, all of them, don't just get awarded for one good race, one lucky day. They are for consistency, for hard work, for doing your best on good and bad days. For keeping on running, even if you don't know why or how, and never giving up. You're all winners, whether or not you're holding a trophy today," says Charlie's dad with a huge smile, after giving out the cups for each age group. "Because you've all given so much to the club this year. And beyond the club, to our community as well." He nods at Auntie Jo, who steps up to the mike.

"Can you hear me okay?" she says. A couple of voices shout back, other people nod or put their thumbs up. "Great, well, I won't take long. I'm Jo and I just wanted to say thank you to everyone who bought cakes and generously donated to my marathon fund, helping the maternity unit. You don't even really know me, but even so you raised hundreds of pounds, just in one morning. I thought of you all when I was running, I knew I couldn't let you down, and after three hours and fifty-seven minutes, I did it!"

She pauses, while people clap. I'm sure I'm clapping the hardest. Except possibly for Mum and Dad. Dad even whoops. "Now, I've just got one more thing to say. You all know Aidan, my nephew. Now he's been on at me for a while about the joys of fell running and how soft I am for sticking to the roads..." There's some laughter. I wonder, what's she going to say now? "And, well, he's right. Now that I've done the marathon, I'm looking for a new challenge. So...I'm going to be back here next season, in the beginner races, getting as muddy as everyone else. I've got all of you to thank for that, but especially Aidan."

I feel a blush spreading up my neck as people look my way. Then Auntie Jo winks at me and I grin back.

OCTOBER

Chapter Twenty-One

We're finally on the way to London. Four adults; seven kids; a mountain of snacks in case we get hungry; travel games, colouring books and phones in case we get bored; and extra layers in case we get cold. And loads of gift bags full of presents. We take up three tables and most of the luggage racks. It's only a two-hour train journey each way. We're coming back this evening because Mum didn't want to leave Toto and Dorothy by themselves overnight.

It's six months since we *didn't* go to London for the marathon, even though we wanted to, but now we're on our way to an event that's even more special.

I tug at my collar, it's stiff and scratchy. "I don't get why you made me wear a shirt," I complain to Mum.

"Justin and Atif said it was an informal do – that I could wear what I felt comfortable in."

"People *always* say that," replies Mum. "But then you get there and find everyone's in their best gear except you. Better to be too smart than to look scruffy. Anyway, it's only for a day, Aidan, and you'll look really good in the photos – very grown up."

I snort, wondering if eight in the morning is too early to crack open the packet of Minstrels lying on the table between me and Jack. I decide that it isn't.

Evie and Daisy loved dressing up for today. They are going through a frilly stage and are both wearing their party dresses, the ones which used to be Chloe's and, before that, belonged to Bells. Neither Chloe nor Bells are wearing dresses today, but they're both still in their best clothes. Mum even pretended not to notice when Bells and Lily came back from the station loos with definite signs of eye make-up and lipstick. On a normal day she'd get Bells to wash it off because she says that Bells isn't old enough for make-up yet.

"Anyway," says Jack, popping a Minstrel into his mouth. "You're going to be centre stage later on. You've got to look your best."

"Don't remind me," I groan. "I *still* don't know what I'm going to read. I don't know why they asked me."

"Neither do I," says Bells. "I'll do it if you don't want to."

"No," says Mum. "They asked your brother, although I wish he hadn't left it to the last minute. You've already got a job anyway, showing people to their seats."

"You've got nothing to worry about, not with me to help you," Jack tells me. He digs in his bag and pulls out a book.

"What's that?"

He holds up the cover to show me.

"A poetry anthology? Who carries their school poetry anthology around with them at the weekend?" I ask.

"Your helpful best mate, that's who. There's *bound* to be something in here for you."

"I don't know, poetry, it's not really my thing. It'll just come out sounding fake."

"No, it won't. Not if we find the right thing. Come on." He starts flicking through the book.

"What do you think it's going to be like today, Laura?" asks Jack's mum, slipping off her heels under the table. "I've never been to a naming ceremony before. I can't get over that they invited me and Jack. I mean, it's not like we're family or anything."

"You're like family to us," interrupts Dad. "Honorary members of the team, eh, Jack? You held the fort while the rest of us were at the hospital."

"Well," says Mum. "I don't know really, but from what they've said, I guess it's a bit like a christening, except not in church and no religious stuff."

"Don't be daft, Mum, of *course* it's not in church," says Bells scathingly. "Atif's Muslim, isn't he? He told me they wanted to do something that included everyone. Anyway, it's not called a naming ceremony, it's a POP."

Mum raises her eyebrows at Jack's mum. "Thinks she knows everything, that one. I like that, POP, Parental Order Party. I think the lads made that name up themselves. It makes it sound fun. I know the legal stuff's important and this parental order from the court is what's made them legal parents, but really that's just a bit of paper telling us what we already know. Today we're here for the party."

"Yeah," says Dad. "I'm ready for a party. Especially since this year's Team Taylor barbecue got rained off for the first time in living memory." I know Mum and Dad will be in their element here, so many new people to meet. I'll be okay because there's enough of us from home that I won't have to talk to anybody I don't know if I don't want to.

Jack keeps pointing out poems for me in his book, but they're all too mushy or too flowery or full of thees and thous, or just don't feel right.

It's not until the train is slowly pulling into London that I find something that just clicks. It's an outdoors poem and I think it's about finding your path. About making decisions – even if you're not sure if they are the right ones. Trying to move forward and not look back, and doing your best. At least, that's what it means to me. I read it over and over again in my head. I can't quite work out whether it's happy or sad or somewhere in between. It's simple and it's complicated all at once, but there's no tricky words to trip me up. It feels like it says all the things I want to say but says them much better than I could.

"What do you think?" I ask Jack. "Will Justin and Atif think it's okay?" Evie and Daisy are pressing their noses to the train windows, watching the platform appear, and Mum and Dad are hassling everyone to clear up their rubbish and not forget their jackets.

Jack reads it through silently while I wait. "Good," he says at last. "Good choice. Justin and Atif trusted you to choose something, didn't they? I'm sure they'll be fine with it. Now let's go. London, here we come..."

Justin told us we should get a taxi, but instead Auntie Jo takes charge and directs us all on and off two buses to get to the hotel. Outside, there's a chalkboard which says "POP" with silver balloons attached and a big arrow pointing to a marquee in the grounds.

"That's us then," says Dad. "Evie, Daisy, trip to the loo before we go in, I think." And he hurries them off into the main hotel building.

We'd timed it to get there early to help, but it looks like everything's almost ready. We spot Justin talking earnestly with one of the hotel staff and gesturing to the area of the marquee where a bar is being set up. Mum taps him on the shoulder. He turns round and, in a split second, his face shifts from worried to warm.

"I can't say how glad I am you're here," he says, enveloping Mum in a huge hug. "All of you."

"So, where is he?" says Mum. "The star of the show."

"Yes," says Auntie Jo. "I'm determined to get a cuddle in before everyone's queuing up for their turn!"

"You might already be too late," says Justin. "He's over there, fast asleep in his grandma's arms. Wish he slept like that at night!" He nods over towards a thin, slightly anxious-looking woman in a big hat, who must be his mum. "I said it was informal, but she insisted on the hat," he says apologetically.

"We'll just go and say hello then," says Auntie Jo, and she and Mum disappear.

Justin turns to Bells. "Can you, Lily and Chloe go and find Atif? He should be right at the back with his two older nephews. You're with them on the welcoming team.

I hope that's okay. It's a really important job and I know you'll be brilliant."

Once they've gone, Justin turns to me. "Are you all right with the reading?"

"Er, yes," I say. "I'm sorry I left it so late. I haven't even told you what I've chosen."

Justin waves a hand. "It's fine. I know it's been busy, start of a new term and everything."

I shove my hands in my pockets. That's not the real reason. I've just been trying to put off thinking about what it will be like standing in front of all those people. If I don't think about it, maybe it will go away. Like that's worked really well for me before.

There's an awkward silence. I've seen Justin loads of times in the last few months, but it's always been in crowded rooms full of noise and chat and other people. Never just me and him. We haven't spoken about the night before the birth, the night I stormed out of the house and ran away.

"Do you want to have a look?" I offer him the book of poems. "Jack helped me choose, so it should be all right, but if you don't like it, we can find something else."

He hesitates for a moment, as if by taking the book he'll be showing that he doesn't trust me.

"Go on," I say.

He takes the book and reads the poem. I shift from side to side, trying to work out his reaction by watching his face.

He nods slowly. "That's right, isn't it? I mean, that bit about taking the less travelled road." He's not looking at me any more, instead his eyes are moving round the marquee, watching the different groups of family and friends arrive and start to mingle and talk to each other. "Atif and I, we *had* to do things differently to make our family. But that meant your mum and dad and all of you going on this strange journey too, without any of us knowing how things would turn out. I know you didn't choose that, Aidan, that you didn't want it. But thank you for doing it anyway."

I feel like this is a time to say something wise and meaningful and grown up, but I can't think what, so I just open my mouth and hope the right thing comes out.

"Sorry," I say. I *am* sorry, but it's a bit of a feeble start. I feel bad when I think about what Atif told me, about how much Justin worries about whether people like him or not, especially when I know how that feels. I certainly gave him something to worry about.

"I didn't make it easy for you. But, you know..." Now, it's my turn to look round the marquee, as I search for the right words, my turn to watch everyone chatting and laughing and gathering round the baby. "I *do* want it," I say quietly. "I choose it now."

Before Justin can reply, Bells appears at his shoulder. "You need to come," she says. "It's urgent. There's someone with a huge cake and they are asking me where to put it and I don't know."

"Right," says Justin. "Let's go." He hands me back the book. "The reading, it's perfect. You chose just the right thing." And he smiles at me and I smile back and I know we're okay.

That doesn't stop me feeling nervous when the ceremony begins, or getting more and more jittery, the longer it goes on. The worst bit is that I'm not on until right at the end. I've got to sweat through the music, the other readings *and* the promises before I can relax. It's far, far worse than waiting for any race to start.

There's a smiley woman in a smart suit who seems to be organizing everything. After welcoming all of us and introducing some music, she invites Justin and Atif to come forward, holding baby Faiz. Faiz is wide awake and, in between gummy smiles, is trying to stick his whole chubby little fist in his mouth. He seems to be relishing the attention. Maybe that's Mum's genes.

Atif steps forward, with one arm round Faiz, who is

balanced on his hip. He reaches out his other hand to hold Justin's.

"Thank you everyone for being here for us and for Faiz, not just today, but during this whole long journey. We've called this event a POP, but it's also a naming ceremony, a chance to formally introduce Faiz Matthew Coleman-Khan to you all. Quite a long name for such a small person."

Faiz starts hiccupping, as if in agreement. A few people laugh. "But there is a meaning behind it, that we'd like to share with you. 'Faiz' and 'Matthew', for those who don't know, both have similar meanings – they both mean 'generous' or 'gift of God'. We chose these names because the only reason we were able to start our own family is because of the incredible generosity of two people, Laura and Pete Taylor, as well as their children Aidan, Bells, Chloe, Daisy and Evie. Thank you, you are like family to us and I hope we are to you."

I look over at Mum. Auntie Jo and Jack's mum are both passing her tissues, one from each side, and she's nodding and sniffing at the same time. Dad is looking straight ahead very firmly.

"There's one more thing. Laura and Pete, I hope you will see this as a tribute, and in the spirit it's meant. We also knew we had to give our son a name that began with

'F' to be part of the Taylor tradition. Faiz is our son, we're his dads, but he will always know his story, and he will always know how special you are to us."

By this time, Mum has given up trying to hold it together and is actually sobbing. Soon she's going to be hiccupping louder than Faiz. It's a relief when Atif stops right there and the smiley woman steps up again to introduce his oldest sister to come and do a reading. I'm not sure we could take any more emotion.

When it's time for me to come forward, I feel sick and my heart is racing. I just hope I don't faint dead away midway through. Not only would it be the most embarrassing thing ever, but I don't think Mum would ever forgive me.

I step up to the mike. I haven't really prepared this bit, so I'm planning to keep it short and just read the poem. "Er, this is for Faiz," I say. "I hope he has a wonderful life, and learns to follow his own path, whatever that will be, just like his dads are doing." I stare at the page. The words swim in front of my eyes, like little black tadpoles, unable to keep still.

I clear my throat and start, "Two roads diverged in a yellow wood…"

Then I stop and look up.

So many people. A mass of faces. I can't do this.

But then I remember Jack and his breathing exercises for *Midsummer Night's Dream*, and I take a deep breath. Then another. In then out again. Individual faces begin to appear out of the blur. Auntie Jo, leaning forward, smiling at me. Mum, still dabbing her eyes with a damp tissue. Jack, his head tilted to one side, looking expectant. Bells, chewing her nails. Dad, rubbing his chin thoughtfully. All of them. All my family and more.

"Two roads diverged…" I start again. And I keep going, loud and strong and without hesitation or stumbling over any of the words, right up until the end.

"…I took the one less travelled by, And that has made all the difference."

After the ceremony's all over, Jack and I find a spot in a quiet corner of the marquee to demolish the plates of food we've piled high at the buffet. We're just scoffing our huge pieces of cake – I feel like I need so much sugar in my system to compensate for all the energy I used up worrying about my reading – when Bells slumps down in a chair next to us.

"Okay, Bells?" Jack asks. "What's up?"

She sighs this huge sigh. "Oh, nothing."

We wait. "Well, all right, it's Lily. All she wants to do is hang out with Zain. I mean, she's *my* friend, she only got invited because of *me* and now she's gone off with him."

"Who's Zain?" I ask.

"Atif's nephew, over there." She nods towards the front of the marquee. I look over. I can see why Lily might want to spend today with Zain instead of with my sister. He's hot. She's flicking her hair over her shoulder and he's leaning in to say something to her. They both laugh.

"Well," says Jack. "Sorry, Bells, you won't see any more of her today, but you can hang out with us if you like. Aidan's refusing to go and talk to anyone, although plenty of random elderly relatives keep coming over and telling him how beautiful his reading was. I reckon he'll be auditioning with us for the school play after that." He makes a dramatic gesture, like he's pretending to wipe away tears of emotion. I make a face at him, although secretly I'm quite chuffed about how well it went.

"Hey," continues Jack. "Has Atif got any more nephews that look like that? Do you reckon there's one for Aidan too?"

"Oh shut up," I say to Jack automatically.

"You've gone bright red!" says Bells gleefully. "You have, you know. Actually, yes, Zain's big brother was doing the welcoming with us as well. He's by the drinks, look. Shall I go and introduce you?"

"Shut up both of you, okay? Sit down, Bells. Stop grinning like that. I don't need your help in finding a boyfriend."

It feels so strange to say the word "boyfriend", especially in connection to me, and not feel like the sky's going to fall in. It's still so embarrassing that I want to crawl in a hole and die, but not because I like boys, but just, well, just because, who I may or may not fancy isn't anyone else's business, is it? But I'm not sure that Jack and Bells would agree. I think they both consider what I do with my life is entirely their business.

"All right then, *you* go over and talk to him, *we'll* stay here," says Jack, with a gleam in his eye.

"No, come on, stop it…" I say. But they are both staring at me. It's a challenge.

"Oh, all *right*," I say. "All right, but this is *stupid*. This is just to shut you both up, okay? Then I'm coming straight back." I stuff a bit more cake in my mouth, the extra energy can't do any harm, and stride towards the drinks before I can think of a million reasons not to. Anyway, it can't be as awkward as that conversation with Will at the barbecue last year. There's no risk of me squirting ketchup everywhere today, that's one thing.

"Hi," I say quickly. I'm standing next to Atif's nephew, but instead of looking at him, I'm staring at my own hands resting on the bar. I just need to get this over with. “Hi, I’m Aidan.” Then I pause and say “hi” again. Oh god.

“I know,” he smiles at me. “Uncle Atif told us about you. I mean, he told us about all your family, and I saw you up at the front earlier. I’m Zak. Uncle Atif said you’re into running, right?” Zak’s got this energy about him when he talks, lighting up his face, his words falling over each other to get out.

“Yeah,” I say. “That’s right.”

“Me too. I’m a sprinter. I love that buzz you get when you just go for it, you know, full on for the finish.”

“I do more long distance,” I say. “Out in the countryside. Have you ever tried it? You still get that buzz though, when you make it through the mud to the top of a really steep hill.”

“No, but maybe I should. Not that there’s many hills round where we live. But, I mean, you’ve got to try everything, haven’t you? No point in being scared you can’t do it, you’ve just got to go for stuff, right? Otherwise you miss out.” He stops, looks at me. “At least, that’s what I think.”

“Yeah,” I say, surprising myself with how definite I sound. “That’s what I think too.”

Out of the corner of my eye, I can see Jack and Bells with their heads together, but I’m too far away to tell whether they are looking at me. I realize with a jolt that I don't care if they are or not. Well, not much anyway.

So many of the things I used to worry about don't seem to matter so much any more. Mum and Dad and Auntie Jo and everyone important knows I'm gay, and nothing's changed. They don't treat me any differently or care about me any less.

And if people at school find out about the surrogacy and think it's weird, well, who cares? Seeing Justin, Atif and Faiz together today makes me understand exactly why Mum wanted to do it. I've even told a couple of people already. I thought Jack was going to choke on his crisps when he heard me explaining to India what we were doing this weekend. She just said it was cool, and asked if I had any cute baby pics on my phone to show her.

I'm starting to realize that it doesn't matter what other people think. Jack's taught me that, Justin and Atif too. I can be who I want to be, whoever that is. I don't have to try to be the same as everyone else. And neither does anyone else.

There's nothing I'm running away from any more.

Acknowledgements

To have one book published is a dream come true. *Just Like Everyone Else* is my third and I'm sure someone's going to wake me up soon. But before they do, there are a lot of people I'd like to thank.

Above all, thank you to Michael, Nick and Sarah for talking me through some of the details of your surrogacy journey and answering my questions. And thank you to all the other families formed through surrogacy who shared their stories with me when I was researching my LGBTQ+ parenting guide, *Pride and Joy*. *Just Like Everyone Else* wouldn't have been possible without you. I hope you feel that I've been true to your experience. Any errors or creative liberties taken are, of course, all mine.

Surrogacy takes many forms. This is just one (fictional) family's story, and it cannot cover every experience. However, it is inspired by Surrogacy UK's model of "surrogacy through friendship" and I have learnt so much from their podcast and information-packed website. Dustin Lance Black's Radio 5 podcast on surrogacy was also extremely useful (you can hear me being interviewed for about 30 seconds in the final episode!) and is highly recommended. I have also learnt a lot over the years from the work of organizations like Hidayah, Imaan and Stonewall, and the people who drive them, which has seeped into *Just Like Everyone Else* without me even realizing.

I'd also like to thank a few individuals who have helped me with getting specific aspects of the story right. Thank you to Conor Cavanagh and Seth Rogers for helping me with some of the interaction between Aidan and Jack by knowing more about gaming than me. Thank you to Sarah Wittams-Howarth for being one of my first readers and always responding within seconds to my WhatsApp questions about secondary school life – it's many years since we lived together in Sheffield, but visiting you there has kept my memories of the city fresh. Thank you to Hamza Jahanzeb for your sensitivity read, bringing an LGBTQ+ Muslim perspective to the story, and a Northern one too!

The team at Usborne have been awesome as ever. I feel so proud to be an Usborne author. Special thanks to Stephanie King for enthusing about this book from the very start and, through her incisive comments and questions, making it so much better by the end, and to Alice Moloney for taking it over the finish line. Thank you to Adamma Oti Okonkwo for her copy-editing skills and Deirdre Power and Gareth Collinson for proofreading. Thank you to Olivia Daisy Coles, Will Steele and Sarah Cronin for making this book look so beautiful! Thank you also to my agent Chloe Seager for always calmly believing that it would all work out, even when I got wobbly.

Three books in, I now know something for sure that I always suspected: teachers, librarians, indie bookshops, Usborne partners and book bloggers are inspirational and amazing people. Thank you for all the work you do in cheerleading for books and getting them into the hands of kids who need them.

It's been wonderful to visit so many schools, both virtually and in-person, to spend time with students and witness their creativity and enthusiasm. What's been most wonderful is seeing someone's eyes light up, or hearing them tell me, or getting an email from a parent or teacher afterwards, because they have seen themselves or their family in one of the stories I'm telling.

And finally, thank you to my friends, who have bought and championed and supported all my books and sent me pictures when you have spotted them in the wild. And to my family – my huge, extended how-do-I-even-explain-how-I-am-related-to-you family – who have all cheered these books on in different ways, but the biggest thanks go to Rachel, Esther, Miriam and my mum for everything and more.

Discussion Questions

1. What did you know about surrogacy before reading this book? What did you learn about it from Aidan's story?
2. What do you think about the title of this book? Does it fit the story?
3. "I'm not into all the things that you're supposed to be into, I mean, if you're gay…Like on Queer Eye, where they're all so well-dressed and loud and over-the-top and all air-kissing and stuff….And I'm into sport. Like, can you be gay and into sport?" How do stereotypes affect the way Aidan sees himself and his sexuality? How do they affect the way people treat him and Jack?
4. When Aidan asks Jack if he's gay, he sends him a text. Why do you think he might do this, instead of talking face to face?

5. Jack says, "I don't get why some things are supposed to be okay for girls and not for boys, or the other way round." Can you think of some examples of things people say are only for one gender? Do you agree?
6. How does running help Aidan cope with his emotions? Do you have something that helps you when you feel overwhelmed?
7. Not everyone in *Just Like Everyone Else* is as accepting as Aidan's friends and family. Why do you think it's important to include characters like Mr and Mrs Evans in a story like this?
8. How does growing up in such a big family affect Aidan? Do you think it makes a difference that he is the only boy?
9. At the end of *Just Like Everyone Else*, Aidan comments that Justin, Atif and baby Faiz "look like a family". What does the idea of family mean to you? How are different ideas of family explored in this book?
10. There are a lot of brave characters in *Just Like Everyone Else*. What do you think is the bravest action in the story, and why?

USBORNE QUICKLINKS

The internet is a great source of information, but it's very important to know which sites you can trust. We have selected useful websites where you can find out more about some of the topics in **Just Like Everyone Else** and these are available at Usborne Quicklinks. Here you can find information about sexuality and gender stereotypes, surrogacy and what LGBTQ+ means, as well as where to go for advice and help.

For links to these websites, go to usborne.com/Quicklinks and type in the title of this book or scan the QR code below.

Please follow the internet safety guidelines at Usborne Quicklinks. Children should be supervised online.

Also by SARAH HAGGER-HOLT

I wonder what people would think if they could take the front off our house, like a doll's house, and watch us. All in the same house, but everyone separate. No one talking, but everyone thinking the same thing. Will we ever be a normal family again?

Izzy's family is under the spotlight when her dad comes out as Danielle, a trans woman. Now shy Izzy must face her fears, find her voice, confront the bullies and stand up for her family.

"Gentle and compassionate." ***The Times Literary Supplement***

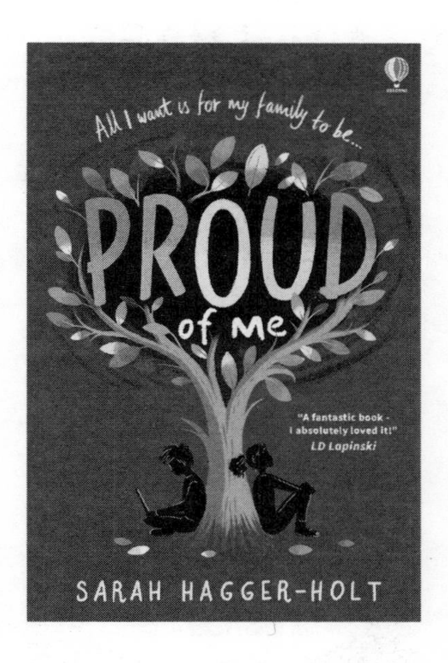

Becky and Josh are almost-twins, with two mums and the same anonymous donor dad.

Josh can't wait until he's eighteen, the legal age when he can finally contact his donor, and he'll do anything to find out more – even if it involves lying.

Becky can't stop thinking about her new friend, Carli. Could her feelings for Carli be a sign of something more?

Becky and Josh both want their parents to be proud of them...but right now, they're struggling to even accept themselves.

"Warm, funny and believable." ***The Guardian***

About the author

Sarah Hagger-Holt is an award-winning and critically acclaimed author. Her debut novel for children, *Nothing Ever Happens Here,* was nominated for the Carnegie Medal, and her second, *Proud of Me*, was the winner of the Little Rebels Award for Radical Children's Fiction. She is the author of two adult non-fiction LGBTQ+ books and has written for the i paper, the Huffington Post, and spoken on Radio 4's Woman's Hour about LGBTQ+ parenting. Sarah lives with her partner and two daughters in Hertfordshire.